THE FRIEND IN NEED

Once Felicity had been foolish enough to think herself in love with Thomas Russell. She had been barely more than a girl then, of course. She had since learned the facts of life and the ways of the world, and knew that Tom and she were meant not to be lovers but only the best of friends.

Naturally, it was Tom to whom she turned for help in her brilliant campaign to force Lord Edmond Waite to ask for her hand in marriage rather than for her person in dalliance. A jolt of jealousy was needed— and the sight of her in Tom's arms would bring the proud lord to heel.

But when Tom took her in his arms, and his lips came down on hers, Felicity began to wonder if she were fooling not the irresistible Lord Waite but her own suddenly divided self. . . .

THE
TRYSTING PLACE

THE
TRYSTING
PLACE

∽⌇∽

Mary Balogh

Ø
A SIGNET BOOK
NEW AMERICAN LIBRARY

NAL BOOKS ARE AVAILABLE AT QUANTITY DISCOUNTS
WHEN USED TO PROMOTE PRODUCTS OR SERVICES.
FOR INFORMATION PLEASE WRITE TO PREMIUM MARKETING DIVISION,
NEW AMERICAN LIBRARY, 1633 BROADWAY,
NEW YORK, NEW YORK 10019.

SIGNET TRADEMARK REG. U.S. PAT. OFF. AND FOREIGN COUNTRIES
REGISTERED TRADEMARK—MARCA REGISTRADA
HECHO EN CHICAGO, U.S.A.

SIGNET, SIGNET CLASSIC, MENTOR, PLUME, MERIDIAN AND
NAL BOOKS are published by New American Library,
1633 Broadway, New York, New York 10019

First Printing, June, 1986

1 2 3 4 5 6 7 8 9

PRINTED IN THE UNITED STATES OF AMERICA

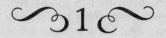

1

For two whole weeks everything that happened in the Maynard household revolved around one fact: Felicity was coming home. The twins had had new muslin dresses for the occasion, made by the village seamstress, not in the newest mode, they feared, when they saw that the copy of the *Belle Assemblée* out of which they had taken the design was more than a year old. But still, the dresses were new, one in primrose, the other in pink because no one, not even Papa in his more absentminded moods, could tell them apart if they wore identical clothing. Felicity would see them at their best and they would convince her of their advanced age and sophistication.

During those two weeks Mr. Maynard spent less time than usual in his office, poring over the estate books, and more out in the stables seeing that the horses were well-groomed, and in the fields seeing that the crops were all planted and the cows and sheep safely in the pasture where they were supposed to be. It was important that Felicity see a prosperous estate when she came home. He would not have her feel that her sacrifice had been in vain. He still felt guilty when he thought of it. Consequently, he tried to avoid thinking of the matter.

Mrs. Maynard enlisted the services of the housekeeper and the gardener. The former helped her take inventory of all the household linens. The second-best sheets and pillowcases would certainly not be good enough, even in the rooms that Felicity was unlikely to see. Everyone's bed was to be made up with the best. And all the table linens were to be changed. Only lace would do, those cloths that she herself had made with her own mama before her wedding. The gardener was instructed to see to it that the lawns were neatly cut, the shrubs trimmed, and the daffodils and tulips in bloom. The poor man scratched his head and looked thoughtful at the last instruction, since in his experience all flowers bloomed when they were ready and died when their time was up. But if Miss Felicity was coming, then he would have to do his best.

The Maynard boys were from home. Cedric was the newly appointed curate of St. Jude's, thirty miles away, and the new husband of the former Miss Bertha Mannering, daughter of a neighboring landowner. It was unlikely that they would come home solely for the purpose of seeing Felicity, but Laura, the more industrious twin, sat down to write them a long letter apprising them of the fact of her sister's visit. She wrote to Adrian as well. It was not that he would choose not to come. Poor boy, he would be wild with eagerness to do just that. But Eton schoolboys are not allowed to go tearing home whenever the spirit moves them. If that were the case, Adrian would not even be a boarder, but a very irregular day pupil, Laura reflected with a smile as she signed her name with a flourish at the bottom of the closely written sheet.

Felicity was coming home after five years. It was a long time. Mr. Maynard had only been beginning to recover when she had left. His stables had still been almost bare, his soil poor, his fences in need of repair, his tenants' houses dilapidated. He had no longer been in danger of ruin, but the improvements had been slow. It was only in the last two or three years, in fact, that his estate had begun to look again like that of a reasonably well-to-do man.

Five years before, Mrs. Maynard had only begun to recover the natural placidity of temper that carried her unscathed through any number of crises. But she had lost it for a few years when she had been convinced that they were all bound for the poorhouse. Her favorite occupation in those days had been to take stock of all the furnishings of the house, all the pictures and linens and china and pots and pans, all the clothes and jewelry they possessed, and list them in the order in which they were to be pawned or sold.

Five years before, Cedric had just gone up to Oxford, and Mrs. Maynard had shed many tears during Felicity's visit over the miracle that had allowed him to go there instead of having to seek employment as a farm laborer or in one of the new factories in some town. Adrian had been only ten years old and already benefiting from the instruction of a strict tutor. Not that Adrian would have considered it a benefit, of course. He had been, and still was, as different from his brother as chalk is from cheese. While the older boy was never happier than when he had his nose in a book, Adrian saw reading and studying as some form of horrific invention to interrupt life. If he could have spent all his days climbing trees or fishing in the stream or riding his horse or mingling with his father's farm laborers, offering help and showing surprising stamina for one so young and gently bred, he would have thought there was no need to die in order to go to heaven.

The twins had been just thirteen, tall and gangly, pigtails swinging to their waists, dresses inevitably torn in more than one place, noisy and unruly. They did their lessons with Adrian and practiced on the pianoforte for half an hour each day and sat with Mama each afternoon to learn all the embroidery stitches that had ever been invented. They sketched and painted in watercolors and were as accomplished at the art as thousands of other girls in England. They still climbed trees with Adrian when there was

nothing else to do and still rode astride when there
was no one to see them and scold. And they were
beginning to nudge each other and giggle whenever
a passably handsome boy moved within their line of
vision, usually at church on Sundays. Many was the
time when the twin who was unfortunate enough to
sit next to Mama was punished with a powerful dig
in the ribs from her elbow.

All four members of the family still living at home
then waited eagerly to show Felicity how things had
changed. Mr. Maynard was now unquestionably comfortable and well-to-do. Farmers for miles around
envied his orderly and prosperous estate. Mrs. Maynard, without being in any way conceited, now
enjoyed the position of leading lady of the neighborhood. She and her family occupied the only padded
pew in the church on Sundays, and her opinion was
always deferred to in any community decision. Her
name always headed the list of guests for any entertainment within miles. It was all most gratifying,
especially when one had a wealthy daughter coming
to visit.

The twins, of course, were bubbling with excitement at having the chance to show their sister just
how grown-up they were—all of eighteen, with
oceans of poise and worldly wisdom between them.
They had a scheme all worked out, which no one
knew of except them. They whispered and giggled
about it frequently, but had promised each other
that they would not breathe a word of it to Felicity—or
anyone else, for that matter—until they were sure
that it would be received favorably.

By the afternoon of the day on which the visitor
was expected, excitement was running high. Mr.
Maynard had made three separate trips to the stables to make sure that the grooms had brushed all
the horses until their coats shone. Mama and the
girls were dressed, the twins in their new muslins,
Mrs. Maynard in her second-best, the gown she
wore to church on Sundays. Cook was in a lather,

having baked four different cakes when she suddenly remembered that each was Miss Felicity's favorite, in addition to preparing a dinner that would
have been more than adequate for a full-scale banquet.

Lady Felicity Wren was trying to relax in the very
comfortable carriage in which she rode alone. If she
had the window up, the interior quickly became hot
and airless. If she lowered it, the dust from the road
stung her eyes and dried her throat. The seat that
she occupied, though of plush velvet and well-sprung,
felt hot and uncomfortable after hours of travel, relieved by only one brief stop for luncheon. She had
tossed aside her bonnet long ago and drawn off her
kid gloves. But she longed to rap on the front panel
and order the footman to let her down so that she
might walk at the side of the road, feeling the cool
grass against her ankles, listening to the chaffinches
in the trees and gathering some of the primroses
from among the hedgerows. Of course, she could
not do so. She was Lady Wren. But it was amazing
how closeness to home could almost nullify the hab-
its of eight years and make her want to behave as
she had as a girl. She sighed.

Five years! It was five years since she had been at
home. She could not quite explain to herself why it
had been so long. She had been in England most of
the time, she supposed, though she and Wilfred had
traveled extensively on the Continent. True, they
had lived in the north, too far from Sussex for a
casual visit, but that was no excuse. They had been
in London for the Season almost every year. She had
always promised herself that she would take a week
off from the busy social round of city life during the
spring and come home. But she had never done so
after the first few years. She had been glad to see
her parents recovering, pleased to know that they
were happy in the knowledge that their home and
position were secure, gratified to see that Papa was
making the effort to improve his estate so that in

future he could be independently affluent. She had been delighted to see the children, to know that their way of life would be preserved for them.

Even so, those early visits had been painful. Their happiness and security had been dearly bought. It was not that she found her life with Wilfred unendurable. In fact, she had a life more full of glamour and variety than she could ever have dreamed of. But when she was home, she was reminded too strongly of the way life had been: simple, routine, happy. And she always had to be enthusiastic during those visits, regaling them with stories about *ton* parties, her presentation to the old queen at St. James's, her visits to Vienna and Rome and Paris. She had to dress in all her most elegant gowns and finery. And all to convince them that she was happy, that, in fact, no sacrifice had been made at all.

All that might have been bearable. She might have continued the visits. But there was that other, too. She had never known when she might run into Tom, and she could not have borne that. And yet, each time when she did *not* run into him, she had returned to London disappointed. Of course, on the first two visits home she had known he would not be there. He was still at university the first time. He was in Europe, making the grand tour the second time. But on the third occasion she had known that he was at home, and she had taken great pains to avoid all the places where he might be, even feigning a headache so that she would not have to accompany her family to church on Sunday.

But that was all behind her now, all of it. For the first time in eight years she felt free, totally free, and she was going to make the most of it. She had every intention of starting to live life to the full, of putting the past behind her, of making up for lost time. She had married Wilfred eight years before. She had made the sacrifice, almost kicking and screaming the whole way, but she had made it. She could remember now the horror she had felt when the elderly

man by whom she had been so repulsed at a birthday ball ten miles away had called on her father the
day after to make an offer for her. She had known
that she was an exceptionally beautiful girl, with her
well-developed figure, thick golden hair, and ivory-
tinted complexion. And she had dressed that night
to dazzle, in a gown of white Brussels lace over a
pink underdress, the brainchild of the village seamstress. But the day after she had cursed her beauty
and her gown. Sir Wilfred Wren wished to marry
her.

The idea should have been ludicrous. The proposal should have become the great family joke. Sir
Wilfred was more than sixty years old; he had never
been married, and he had obviously never been a
handsome man. He had a brash, overconfident manner that Felicity learned later stemmed from a deep
insecurity. Although accepted in all the highest social circles, he did not fit there naturally. He was
what was known as a cit, a man who had made his
money in trade. The fact that he was accepted at all
was due entirely to the fact that he was enormously
wealthy.

This last fact had spelled Felicity's doom. Her father, at the time, had been on the verge of financial
ruin. There seemed no way by which he could hold
off his debtors much longer. His rather large family
faced a bleak future indeed. Sir Wilfred Wren had
seemed like a gift sent from heaven. For some reason he had decided that he wanted Felicity very
badly. He was willing to pay a very high price.
Money meant little to him, anyway, now that he
possessed so much of it. Mr. Maynard, and later his
wife, had begged and pleaded with her. It was true
that she was very young, true that Tom Russell was
likely to offer for her as soon as his studies were
completed, true that Wren was an elderly man. But
could she bear to see her family ruined, to share that
ruin herself, when she had it in her power to save
them all, to set her father back on his feet?

Felicity had cried and agonized over her decision, had sobbed and wailed for Tom, who was away at university, but had known that really there was no decision to make. There was only the question of reconciling herself to the inevitable. So she had done it. At the age of eighteen, she had married a sixty-two-year-old man and gone away with him. She could not complain. He had clearly doted on her, had showered her with gifts, had clothed her only in the best, had decked her with jewels and taken her all over England and Europe, showing her off to the highest society wherever they went. He had been kind. But she had to admit in the privacy of her own coach that it felt good to be free. Wilfred had died one year before of a heart seizure. They had been in Rome. His valet had found him dead beside the bed one morning when he had taken his shaving water in to him. Felicity had brought the body home for burial and had spent her year of mourning with her sister-in-law, Beatrice, a spinster in her fifties, who had devoted much of her life to caring for her brother.

Now Felicity was free. She had taken off her gray gown for the last time two days before when she retired to bed. Yesterday morning, when she had left for her father's home in Sussex, she had dressed in a blue gown that Wilfred had bought for her in Italy. Today she wore green. And she felt as though a great load had been lifted from her back. She had kissed Beatrice good-bye yesterday morning and set out alone on her journey. Her sister-in-law had been distressed that she would not take even a maid, especially when it was imperative that she spend a night on the road, but Felicity had insisted on traveling alone. No longer did she intend to be shackled in any way at all. She was six-and-twenty and extremely wealthy. If she wished to travel alone and stay at an inn alone, then she would do so.

She began to recognize landmarks. Five years began to seem a long time again. Would things be changed? From Laura's letters and the occasional ones from Lucy and Mama, she gathered that the estate was prospering. It would be intriguing to see the twins again. They were grown up, the age she had been when she married Wilfred. Would they have lost the rather ramshackle appearance they had had at the age of thirteen? The pigtails surely would have gone. Would they still giggle? Would she be able to tell them apart?

For the first time in eight years she would be able to enjoy home. Perhaps seeing them all happy would help her remember that the previous eight years had not been in vain. But, oh, sometimes it felt so awful to know that she was six-and-twenty already and had never had a chance to be really free. She gave herself a mental shake. She had also seen places, met people, and done things that many a fifty-year-old would give a right arm to have experienced. She must not complain.

She would be able to enjoy this visit in another way, too. After eight years she was no longer afraid to meet Tom. In fact, she looked forward to doing so. In those years she had finally worked Tom out of her system. She would not go so far as to say that she was glad that Wilfred had appeared to prevent their marriage, but she was nonetheless glad that she had not married Tom. If her married life had taught her one thing, it was that life has a great deal to offer. With Wilfred she had seen so much that had filled her with longing. She had been a part of all these things and yet somehow excluded. She had been a married woman with a very possessive husband. She had been aware, early in her marriage, that members of the *ton*, even the ladies, frequently lived their own lives married to one person for the sake of convenience and social status, but carrying on almost open affairs with others. Such people lived gay and carefree lives. Yet she had never been able to join their ranks. It might have been possible to get away from Wilfred sometimes, but she could never bring herself even to flirt with any other man, let alone be unfaithful.

Yet she had yearned for that other life. And she knew that it was within her grasp. She now owned an elegant mansion on Pall Mall and had so much money that she need never hesitate about buying a new dress or carriage or jewel. She was still young enough to be desirable, and she knew, without vanity, that she was still beautiful. Perhaps more so than she had been at eighteen. She had acquired poise since then and fashion sense. She knew that men found her attractive. Every Season someone new had tried to charm her into his bed, and she had always been as much besieged with partners at a ball as the newest, prettiest debutante. She knew all this and now she was free to participate in that life. After her two-week visit home, she would be moving on to London, where she intended to have the gayest, most dazzling Season that any woman ever had. She was going to find herself a young, handsome, intelligent, wealthy, charming man of rank and she was going to marry him. The very proper Lady Wren, whom men had desired as a mistress while pitying her as a wife, was going to make the most brilliant match of the Season. She would be married in St. George's, Hanover Square, and all the *ton* would be invited. Then she would live the rest of her life in the forefront of social life. She was going to be compensated handsomely for eight irksome years.

Yes, she was very glad she had not married Tom. When she had last seen him, he was twenty years old, but already he had had the maturity and strength of character of an older man. He knew exactly what he wanted of life and Felicity did not think he would have changed his mind. At least the chance mentions of him that were made in letters from home suggested that he was living true to plan. He had gone to university and had studied conscientiously. Tom had always believed that knowledge was valuable in itself. Even if he did intend to spend his life in the country running his father's estate, his mind

could be free to roam the universe, he used to say.
He had always read prolifically. His plan had been
to come home, take over the management of the
estate from his elderly father, marry Felicity, and
settle down to produce a large family.

He had not done several of those things. He had
not immediately settled down, but had traveled for
more than a year. He had not married or produced a
family. But he had taken over from his father and, in
fact, had become owner of the property when his
father had died three years before. His mother was
long deceased. Felicity gathered from the snippets of
news that she pieced together that he was a very
skilled manager. His lands were prospering, at least
as much as her father's were. And this very fact
proved to her that Tom had not changed. He would
be content to spend the rest of his life here in the
country. And she shuddered at the thought that she
might have been trapped here with him. Eight years
with Wilfred had been hard to bear. A lifetime with
Tom would surely have been worse once the glamour of their love had worn away with custom.

She was looking forward to seeing him. She was
curious to look at him and try to recall why she had
harbored such a passion for him and why she had
grieved for him for more than three years after her
marriage. She would surely find him dull and staid
now. She would even be embarrassed to remember
some of their times together, words they had spoken, kisses they had shared, especially that last one
when he had come rushing home from Cambridge.
. . . It would be good to see him again for what he
was, a dull, good-natured farmer, no doubt, eras
removed from her own experience. He represented
the final little piece of her past that would have to be
put in its place before she could turn wholeheartedly
to the future.

Oh, it was good to be alive. Felicity lowered the
windows and breathed in the smells of spring along
with the dust. Soon now! Over the next rise she

would be able to see the house. She leaned forward, her head partly outside the window, heedless of the fact that the wind was detaching wisps of golden hair from her careful chignon. And there it was, finally: the house itself and the stables, looking dearly familiar, surprisingly unchanged; the long lawns sloping away to the south, bordered by beds of gold and varying shades of pink—her mother's pride and joy: the daffodils and tulips, of course—and east of the lawn, the large thicket and the stream, a paradise to her and Cedric and Tom when they were children, a lovers' tryst when she grew older. It was there, yes, just there, under the shade of that oak tree where she had last met Tom, the night before her wedding, where. . . . But never mind that. It was all ancient, rather charming history. The memory no longer had the power to cause pain, only a sweet pull of nostalgia.

Felicity's head suddenly shot completely through the window and with it her right arm. Dignity and sophistication and her six-and-twenty years were forgotten as she waved her arm vigorously to the figures gathered on the small cobbled courtyard in front of the house. Then they disappeared from view as the carriage descended the dip that led to the stone gateway and the driveway that curved up to the house.

Mama was there, looking not a day older, looking for all the world as she always had when ready to go to church. Papa was in the background, hands clasped behind his back, looking quite self-possessed, but with a smile lurking at the corners of his mouth. And the twins caused her to laugh out loud. They looked like coiled springs but were very obviously making an effort to appear ladylike. My, what beauties! And, for heaven's sake, which was which?

"Felicity!" one of them shrieked, and they both stampeded toward the carriage door.

2

Tom Russell sat in a worn leather chair beside the log fire that he had lit against the evening chill. One elbow was propped on the armrest, his hand supporting the side of his head. One booted leg was thrown over the other arm of the chair. He had not dressed for dinner. Sometimes he did so, but it really seemed a pointless effort unless he was receiving company or going out afterward. An almost full glass of port stood on the walnut table beside him, but he had not touched it in a long while. Once he had been very drunk for three days in a row and the sobering-up process had been very painful. And it had all been pointless. The drink had dulled the pain for a few days, but that pain had had to be faced at the end of it all. Since that experience, Tom had always drunk sparingly, especially when he had something on his mind. He now preferred to face his problems head-on, relying only on his brain and his own emotional stamina to help him through to a solution.

She would be home now, surely. It took two days to travel from Yorkshire, but it would have been worked out that she would not have to travel after dark. And darkness had definitely fallen. Tom's eyes wandered to the window, across which the heavy drapes had not yet been drawn. She would be a mere two miles away, sitting at home, doubtless,

17

talking and laughing with her family. Not that it
would make any difference to him, of course. She
might as well be two hundred miles away.

He wondered what she would be like now. Eight
years! It was eight years since he had seen her last,
and that had been a hurried, pained meeting at
night. It was almost nine since he had really talked
to her, spent time with her. Would she still be as
vital and full of mischief as he remembered her? He
knew she was still as beautiful. Not that he had seen
her himself. He had studiously avoided doing so, in
fact. He had once left Vienna the day after his arrival, having heard quite by chance that she was
there with her husband. But he had heard about
her. Her beauty and her aloofness had made her
quite famous. It was not difficult to find a group of
men talking about her. Aloofness! That was one
description of her that Tom found difficult to believe. The Felicity that he knew was anything but
aloof.

Eight years. It was such a long time. She would
have forgotten him, or at least relegated him to the
dim past, just part of her childhood memories. And
why should she not? She had lived a full and varied
life. He did not know how she had got along with
Wren. Tom had seen her husband only once—an
elderly man who had decided on whim that he
wanted a young wife. But Tom had never heard ill
of him. In fact, gossip had it that he doted on her,
lavished his wealth on enhancing her beauty. Perhaps she had been happy. Perhaps she truly mourned
Wren's loss.

Tom would hardly have it otherwise. It was far
too late for them now, even if she still retained some
affection for him. In eight years she would have
become accustomed to the life of glitter and excitement that she had lived. He could not offer her that,
even if he had the money to do so. He belonged
here in the country, managing his estate. He could
not live otherwise for very long, not even for her

sake. He had to be his own person and live his own kind of life or ultimately he would make any woman unhappy, even if he loved her. Tom had learned this about himself in a year and a half of travel. He had seen every important city of Europe, visited cathedrals, museums, and art galleries, mingled with society. And he was not sorry that he had done so. Any experience was an enrichment to life and he felt a wiser and a better-educated man for his travels. He had also learned a great deal about himself. He had learned who he was and where he belonged.

Tom felt himself to be a levelheaded, reasonably mature adult. But only reasonably mature. It was not a fully adult attitude to harbor a hopeless love for eight years. Yet that was just what he had done. And he had learned to accept the fact that he would always love Felicity, that he would never love another woman in the same way. He had tried. During his last year at university and during the first eight months in his travels, he had lived a life of frantic debauchery, trying desperately to drown out his love by performing over and over again and with a dizzying number of partners the mere physical act of love. It had not worked. Never once had he felt a spark of anything more than sheer lust for the woman he bedded.

Well, once perhaps, and she had been in many ways his savior. He had spent two whole weeks with the same little French actress. She was pretty and unusually satisfactory as a bedfellow. Yet, when the time came to leave Paris, he would have kissed her good-bye and given her no further thought. He had been quite taken aback and severely shaken when she had clung to his lapels and cried into his neckcloth, not just sentimental tears, but deep, painful sobs. She had had only one lover before him, she had explained, and that man had taken her only once, by force. She loved Tom. She begged him to stay with her or to let her go with him.

Tom had sat down with her and had talked with

her for several hours. She was the first woman since Felicity that he had really talked to or seen as a person. He had left her at the end of that time, and ironically, that was the first unselfish move he had made in a long time. It was tempting to agree to take her with him, to soothe with her his bruised heart, but he knew that he could never love her. And the longer she spent with him, the more hurt she would be when the liaison came to its inevitable end. But Tom had brooded for days over his own power to hurt another human being. He had forgotten that women had feelings too, not just bodies to be used for one's pleasure.

He had not slept with a woman since that time. And he had accepted the fact that he would never marry, never have the large family that he and Felicity had planned. Six children, it was to be. She had to outdo her mother by one. Well, Tom thought now, lowering his leg from the arm of the chair in order to push a log more firmly onto the fire, perhaps it was just as well. He had become accustomed to his own solitariness, especially since the death of his father. He was no hermit. He frequently dined out and attended any social function that happened within a radius of twenty miles. He sometimes entertained at his own house. And he frequently went during an evening to the local inn, not to drink, but to share news with other men and perhaps to play a hand of cards. He was not at all sure now that six children in the house would be easy to cope with. He smiled. Of course, they would not all have arrived in the snap of a finger. He would have had a chance to get used to them one at a time, or perhaps two at a time. There were twins in Felicity's family.

His love had mellowed. There had been a time when he was ready to kill himself. He still hated to look back on the morning when he had received her letter. He had been on his way to write an examination. He had not failed the test, but he must have come very close. He had rushed home afterward, not stopping to ask permission to return home during term time or even to tell anyone that he was going. And until he was home, he had not realized how irrevocable was her decision to marry Sir Wilfred Wren. The plans were all made, the guests invited. The ceremony was to take place the following day. Tom knew reality then. He knew he could not stop her.

His father had advised him not to try to see her. The elder Russell, a kindly man himself, had realized some of the pain the girl must be suffering. It was general knowledge that Maynard was so close to ruin that recovery was almost impossible. It was equally generally known that Wren had more money than he knew what to do with. It did not take much imagination to work out that Maynard's eldest daughter was to be the sacrificial lamb. And she would not change her mind, father explained to son. She could not. Her whole family depended upon this marriage.

Tom had acquiesced . . . almost. He had not tried to see her. But during the evening he had gone to the oak tree by the stream on her father's estate, their old trysting place. He had not expected her to come, but she had appeared suddenly, quite late. Tom could not be certain now, it was too long ago, but he was almost certain that they had said nothing to each other at first. They had just hugged each other despairingly, her head on his shoulder, his against her cheek, for long, endless minutes. When she had finally lifted her head, they had looked into each other's eyes, darkened in the gloom of late evening, words quite unnecessary. All the misery and hopelessness of their situation had been in that look.

Then he had begun to kiss her, desperate, passionate kisses on her mouth, her eyes, her throat. And she had kissed him back, clinging to him as if for very survival. They had murmured words of love over and over again. They had ended up on the ground, Tom remembered, her back against the hard soil that she seemed not to feel, his weight pinning her there. Then he had done what he had never done with her before. He had pulled with fevered fingers at the laces that held her bodice closed and her full breasts had been released into his hands. Tom had never had a woman; she had never been touched by a man. Blind instinct had sent him to caressing and kissing, her to moaning and arching against him.

His hands had gone under her skirts, pulling and jerking at them until they were bunched around her waist. She had parted her legs and lifted her hips so that he might remove her undergarments. Her own hands had gone to the waistband of his breeches and the buttons that held them closed.

When he had stopped suddenly, the backs of his knuckles against her hips, his fingers down inside the silk next to her skin, she had looked into his eyes and cried out frantically, the first intelligible words that either of them had spoken.

"No, Tom, no, please don't stop! Please!" she had said. "I want you to have me, Tom. I want you to be the first. Please, my love. Oh, please!"

He had collapsed on top of her, his whole weight pinning her against the hard ground. And he had buried his face against her neck and cried. Passion had gradually died between them as love and tenderness held them in warm embrace. His tears soaked her neck and ran unheeded into the valley between her naked breasts. She had not cried.

He had pushed himself to his feet finally and turned his back on her while she brushed her skirts out and confined her breasts within her bodice. Then he had turned back to her. They had not touched again. She had tried to smile. She had tried to say something. But her face was out of her control. She had turned away and began to walk back toward her father's house. The last he had seen of her!

Tom tried to forget that scene as much as he

could, though the memory had mellowed with time. It could still cause a dull ache, but no longer that raw, gut-wrenching pain that he had had to live with for several years.

He loved her, yes. But he believed he could see her again now without causing himself unnecessary pain, without wearing his heart on his sleeve. It would take some courage to walk over there and present himself, but he would do it—tomorrow or the next day, perhaps. He would see her and talk to her, find out how much she had changed and how much she was still the same. He would let her see that he had settled into a placid and dull life, and that he was content with his lot. And then he would come back home and assess the situation, find out if he loved her more or less than he thought now. Perhaps seeing her again would make him realize that he had loved a dream all these years. Perhaps she would be that much changed.

However it was to be, he would be able to relax again having once seen her. He would not seek her out after that, but he would be able to bear with equanimity the occasional meetings that were bound to occur if she spent more time at home now that she was widowed. Yes, tomorrow he would go.

Felicity was dizzyingly busy on her first day at home. Everyone wanted to claim her attention. Papa wanted to take her all over his estate and see the improvements, to see how prosperous it had all become. And she obliged him. Before luncheon she followed him to the stables and duly admired the renovated buildings and the well-groomed mounts within. She asked him to saddle her a fairly quiet horse, and when her father looked at her in surprise, she explained that Wilfred had not liked to see her ride. He had feared constantly for her safety. And her sister-in-law had not thought it appropriate for her to ride during her year of mourning. She needed time to become a practiced horsewoman again.

Together she and Papa rode around much of the estate, viewing the newly seeded fields, the smart fences around the enclosures that had been made since her time, the laborers' cottages, quite new, neat, and sanitary, one of the tenant farmers' homes. Felicity was greeted by several people and discovered, when she looked more closely, a remembered face. It felt good to be back, and good to know that her father had not squandered or misused the money he had acquired from her marriage. She smiled fondly at him as they rode back to the house.

Her mother wanted to show her the house and garden. The daffodils and tulips were easy to remember. She always associated them with spring at home. But now they grew in even greater profusion than they had when she was a girl. The house was much the same, except for a new picture here, a freshly upholstered chair there, and new draperies somewhere else. But Felicity had to see it all.

"Did we have a pianoforte when you were last here?" Mama asked, as she had asked about a dozen other times. "But, yes, of course, we must have. I distinctly remember the twins playing for you on it. And it was not the harpsichord, because I remember thinking how much more mellow the tone was, and what a pity it was that we had not had it when you learned. Your musical talent was always superior to that of any of my other children. Do you still play, my love?"

Felicity smiled, sat at the instrument, and played a short fugue. She did not exaggerate her own talent. Wilfred had liked her to play for him on those evenings when no activity took them from home, and thus she had stayed in practice. But she always declined to play in public. Most ladies, Felicity found, performed with deplorable lack of real talent, and she had no wish to join their numbers.

Throughout the day the twins grabbed her whenever it seemed that she might be approaching a moment of idleness. She was dragged into the morning room by Laura, who pulled an untidy pile of letters from the escritoire and proceeded to read her sister long extracts from letters written by Cedric and Adrian.

"You will be able to see Adrian when you go to London, will you not?" the girl asked her sister eagerly. "He will be so pleased if he can spend an afternoon with you occasionally, or even a weekend. The poor boy does hate school so, Felicity. He says that one day he will run the estate, when Papa grows too old. It is unlikely that Cedric will wish to do so as he will have his own living within the next few years, no doubt. Anyway, Adrian says that he doesn't need to know what Antony said in his market speech in *Julius Caesar*, or the order in which Odysseus experienced his adventures in *The Odyssey*. They won't help him farm, he says. And I must say that I see his point, don't you, Felicity?"

Her sister smiled. "Indeed, it does seem hard at the time to understand why one needs an education," she said. "But think how ignorant we would all be, Lucy, if we learned only those things in life that we need for survival. We would hardly need our human minds."

"You sound just like Mr. Russell," Laura said disapprovingly. "And I am Laura."

Lucy dragged Felicity upstairs to examine her wardrobe. "We really have nothing that is fashionable," she explained, "but Mama says there is no need to be forever buying new clothes when we live so far from town. But you must tell us how dreadfully outmoded they are. This is the one I wore to Hannah Jennings' birthday party two months ago. I was quite pleased with it. Certainly Mr. Moorehead—he is the new curate—took far more notice of us than he did of her. We think he has a *tendre* for one of us, but the thing is, you see, he can never decide which of us it is that he likes."

Her twin in the background giggled.

"It is a pretty gown," Felicity said, holding the

pale-blue dress by the high waist and examining the neckline. "I'll wager you would turn a few heads with that even in London, Lucy. You *are* Lucy, aren't you?"

Both twins giggled.

None of the family ventured beyond the bounds of their own land that day, and no visitors arrived. Felicity was a trifle disapppointed. She thought that for old times' sake Tom might have made an effort to come and pay his respects. Surely he could not have forgotten her entirely. Surely he did not bear a grudge. She hoped that she would see him at least once during her two weeks at home. Being here again reminded her strongly of the deep friendship they had shared for years before they had started to think of each other differently. Already life at home seemed to be missing that one ingredient. They had forever lived in each other's houses as youngsters. There would be no harm in renewing the friendship, would there, now that all the charged feelings and embarrassment of the other had passed quietly into history?

He came on the following day. Felicity was in the garden watching her mother cut some blooms for the house. She was hatless and wore no cloak over her sprigged-muslin dress. It was one of those perfect spring days when the air was hot yet held all the freshness of the new season.

She saw him coming, striding across his own pasture, ducking underneath a fence, and climbing the slight rise that lay between his own land and her father's house. She watched unmoving, eager, curious, a little shy. He was unmistakably Tom, she had known that at a glance when he was still quite a distance away. The purposeful yet somehow carefree stride could belong to no one else. He was dressed rather conservatively in a brown coat, buff riding breeches, and black topboots. Yes, he had always dressed in much the same way. He had not grown at all, but then, why should he? He had been twenty years old when she last saw him. He was not tall, only a few inches above her height, in fact. She remembered the year when he had been quite out of sorts over the fact that a spurt in her growth took her past him for a while. He looked very much the same Tom.

As he drew closer, she became aware of subtle changes. His hair was longish and waved back from his face in no particular style. He had had a queue tied back with a black ribbon when he had gone away to university. When he came back for the first vacation, he had had his hair cut into a very short Brutus style. But it had not suited him. This did. When she had last seen him, he was slender and very boyish in figure. Now he was quite solidly built, and it looked more like muscle than fat that filled out his coat at shoulders and chest and his riding breeches at the calves. Tom had very definitely improved with age.

His eyes caught and held hers for a moment before he lowered his head to watch his step again as he climbed the rise. Still the same steady gray eyes, but not dancing with merriment as they had used to do most of the time. The same pleasant, though by no means handsome face, though the mouth was in repose, not curved into a smile as it had used to be so often.

Felicity did not realize that she had been holding her breath until he circled around a tulip bed and stepped onto the lawn close to her and her mother. No more than two minutes could have passed since she first spotted him striding across the field, yet it had seemed a lifetime.

"Good day to you, Mrs. Maynard," he said in a pleasant, even voice. "Hello, Flick. It's good to see you again." He held out a steady hand to shake hers.

Felicity was in shock. Flick! She had completely forgotten the old pet name that he had given her when they were mere children. She had forgotten

the very attractive trick he had of smiling with his
eyes even when the rest of his face was immobile.
And she had forgotten until her hand went into his
what strong and reassuring hands he had. They had
often walked hand in hand when they were young,
usually swinging their arms as they went.

"Hello, Tom," she said, and suddenly smiled dazzlingly at him. "It's good to *be* home." She hesitated
a moment, her hand still resting in his. Then she
drew a deep breath, flung her arms around his neck,
and pressed her cheek against his. "Oh, Tom, it *is*
good to be back," she said, "and to see you again.
My dearest friend!"

Tom's arms, in a reflex action, had locked behind
her waist. When she leaned away from him to smile
into his face, she thought for one moment that he
was going to kiss her. Instead, he grinned broadly.

"Hoyden!" he said. "The same old Flick!"

"And now that you smile," she said, disengaging
herself from his arms, "I can see that you are the
same old Tom."

She felt enormously relieved. It was just as if the
years had rolled back, beyond her years with Wilfred and beyond the year when she and Tom had
shared a young love. He was as friendly and as dear
as he had ever been, no hint of what they had
briefly been to each other in his face, voice, or manner. He was just gentle, kindly, dependable Tom, to
whom she had always been able to talk as if he were
her other self.

She linked her arm in his, waited until her mother
had gathered together the bundle of flowers in one
hand and the shears in the other, and began to stroll
with him back to the house.

"Tell me all about yourself, Tom," she said eagerly, "and all that you have been doing in the last
years. Oh, what a foolish thing to ask! If there is one
thing best designed to make a person tongue-tied, it
is the direction to tell another person all about one-
self. Tell me anything. Talk to me. Oh, I have so

much to tell you, Tom. You must come over often before I leave for London. I shall make you sorry that you were ever blessed with ears. Will you come, Tom?"

He laughed across at her, and, yes, she remembered those very white, even teeth that would look even more sparkling later in the year when his face became suntanned.

"You had better stop to take a breath, Flick," he said. "Of course I shall come as often as you wish, and you may bare your soul to me. But I insist on equal time. Right now I am trying to find a moment to compliment your mother on those lovely blooms. Why is it that mine always look pale and droopy in comparison, ma'am?"

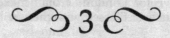

3

It proved to be a blissful two weeks for Felicity. Everyone and everything seemed to have conspired to ensure that her homecoming should be perfect. The weather cooperated. No one could remember a spring when the sun had shone so consistently and so warmly this early in the year. Yet there had been rain enough during the previous months to set the grass to growing and the leaves to budding and the spring flowers to blooming.

Felicity wandered over every part of her father's estate, sometimes on horseback, sometimes on foot, sometimes in company, but many times alone. Her wanderings resulted in a delightful combination of new discoveries and old memories revived. The lower meadow was still used to pasture sheep, she found. The fence was spanking new, but her old friend the wooden stile was still there. It had a broad, flat top that made an excellent seat, and was sheltered from the afternoon sun by a thick hawthorne bush. It had been her favorite hideaway, the place where she came sometimes to think, at other times to read.

The laborers' cottages were new and neatly arranged into a little village of their own. She had seen that the first morning when she had ridden with her father. But many of the occupants were old friends, she discovered when she paid a more leisurely visit on foot a few days later. Old Lionel was sitting in the doorway of one small cottage, a toothless smile on his face. He was retired from active work now, but she remembered the times when he had pressed some of the ears of wheat into her child's hand during harvest so that she might chew on the sweet grain. And Mrs. Parsons bustled out of the house next door when she heard Felicity talking, looking not one day older or one ounce slimmer. Before she had a chance to say a word, Felicity was inside the neat and clean little cottage, a mug of cider and a currant cake on the table in front of her. It was just the same as it had always been, except that it had used to be warm milk rather than cider.

The thicket and the stream were the same as ever, except that the old bridge had finally collapsed. But then it had never been used, anyway, within Felicity's memory. It had always looked too ramshackle to bear anyone's weight, and it was easier merely to gather one's skirts above one's ankles, take a run, and jump across the stream if one really wanted to get to the other side. She visited this area alone. It brought back so many sweet memories. It had provided a magic playground for her and Cedric and Tom when they were children. There were so many trees to climb and places to hide. There was a stretch of grass on which to relax or play ball. There was the stream to jump or wade in. It had been an idyllic childhood. Even the more painful memories could draw a smile now. There had been that time she had fallen into the stream, pushed, she knew, though she never had found out whether it was Cedric or Tom who was the culprit. Neither would confess, and both had rolled around on the ground clutching their stomachs from the pain of laughing so hard. She had left them there and fled to the house, bawling for Mama.

She wandered to the large oak tree and walked all around it, running her palm over the rough old bark. She gazed up into the branches that had so often held three shouting, laughing children. And she thought as she stroked the bark almost lovingly of the kisses she and Tom had shared here in this spot. Fumbling, tender, and chaste kisses all of them except that last. She gazed curiously at the ground before her. Just there she had lain with him. She was half-amused, half-embarrassed at the memory of herself pleading with him, begging him to make love to her. She had been so convinced at the time that nothing else in life beyond that moment would be worth living, so convinced that love was all that mattered in life and that Tom embodied that love for her.

The sweet innocence of youth! What a good thing it was that he had restrained himself at the last moment. She might have felt herself forever bound to him if he had once possessed her person. And what a blessing in disguise it had been, really, that Wilfred had come along. Her years with him had not been really happy ones, but she had learned during those years what life had to offer. She had learned that love did not really matter, that money and rank and the willingness to reach out for pleasure were the important things. Her life now would be so dull if she had not been forced to marry Wilfred: Tom, and probably a good many of their six children already, the countryside, and the occasional entertainment that the neighborhood offered. Very dull!

Not that she did not love Tom, of course. She had been genuinely delighted to see him again. She had felt finally at home when he had come that first time. Only then did she realize how much she had missed his kindly manner, his gently smiling eyes, his friendship. Now that she had found him again, she determined never to lose him. He had been cheerful and friendly on that first visit and on each one since. It was clear that he felt as she did. There was no spark left of that passion that had flared between them for less than a year. They were both ready now for a mature friendship.

True to his word, Tom came every day after that

first visit. Sometimes it was a very brief call, sometimes longer. Once he stayed for dinner and sat on for the rest of the evening. He and Felicity talked a great deal, frequently alone. They exchanged opinions of the many places they had both visited, works of art they had seen, books they had read, people they both knew. They reminisced about their childhood, shared their plans and dreams for the future. It was all marvelous. Felicity had always found Tom to be one of those rare persons with whom one can talk constantly without conscious effort. Cedric had been like that too until his thoughts had turned more and more to the church. He was closer to the Nonconformists than to the Anglican church, Felicity had told him scornfully on one occasion. He had begun to frown on her delight in pretty clothes and parties. They were friends now, exchanged letters at least twice a year, but without the closeness that she still felt with Tom.

Felicity confided to her friend her plans for the future. "I am going to have a marvelous Season, Tom. I am so completely free, you see. The new debutantes have to be careful of every word they speak, every move they make. Their whole reputation depends upon it. And they must be watched every moment of the day. There are definite advantages of being six-and-twenty and a widow."

"No chaperone, Flick?" he asked.

"No, indeed," she said. "Beatrice offered to come with me, though I know it would be a great sacrifice to her to do so. She is my sister-in-law, you know. But I said no. I am far too old to scandalize people by being alone, and I really could not bear to have a chaperone or even a companion. The house in town is very well staffed. I shall have a housekeeper and butler and numerous maids, footmen, and all the rest to add propriety to my situation."

"You like all that dining and dancing and partying, then?" Tom asked.

"Oh, yes, enormously," she replied, "though I never really had a chance to enjoy myself to the full when Wilfred was alive. We went out a lot and entertained frequently, but he liked me to stay close to him. He did not disappear into the card room at a ball as most of the other husbands did."

"Were you very unhappy with him?" he asked quietly.

"Oh, no, not at all." Felicity flashed him a smile. "He was very kind and generous, you see. But a trifle dull, Tom. Next time I intend things to be quite different."

"Next time?"

"Yes," she said. "Next time my husband will be dazzling. Handsome, wealthy, of high rank. Someone who loves traveling and gaiety."

"Do you have anyone in mind?" Tom asked.

"Not yet," she admitted, "but I shall look around me when I get to London. I shall not be in any hurry. I do not intend to make a mistake because this man must also be young, you see, and I might be bound to him for a lifetime. I shall have to be careful to sift out all the fortune-hunters. There are bound to be plenty of those as I am extremely wealthy, you see. Wilfred left almost everything to me."

"What about love?" Tom said. "Won't you have to find a man you can love?"

Felicity gazed fondly at her friend and laughed. "No," she said. "How quaint you are, Tom. Looking for love would be the worst possible way to choose a husband. One has to use one's head, not one's heart. He would, of course, have to be someone I *like* if I am to spend a lifetime with him. Perhaps love will grow. Certainly, I would hope that affection will develop. I should be content with that."

Tom merely smiled and continued to stroll beyond the stables to the small lake that was among the trees. He and Felicity frequently walked out, never planning the direction in which they would go, but always, by tacit consent, avoiding the thicket, the stream, and the oak tree.

"And what about you, Tom?" she asked, peering into his face with an impish grin. "It is time you thought of marriage. You are eight-and-twenty already, quite approaching your dotage. What type of a wife do you mean to choose? Or do you have someone picked out already? If so, she must be getting thunderous over the fact that you spend so much time here with me. However, tell her not to fret. I shall be gone again in one week."

Tom laughed. "I wonder you do not have the marriage ceremony all arranged for me too, Flick," he said. "Unfortunately, my dear, there would be one essential element lacking: a bride. No, I am not in search of a wife. I quite grew into my bachelorhood when Papa was still alive, and I find now that I am too comfortable and too lazy to change my estate. You may continue to claim me as your dearest friend without fearing that the next female you meet may try to claw your eyes out."

"Ah, but that is a shame, Tom," Felicity said. "You are wasting a life. There is so much excitement to be participated in if one just reaches out for it."

"There speaks the voice of youth," Tom teased. "In two years' time, when you are my age, my dear, perhaps you too will be content to slip into a quiet and dull old age."

"Fiddle!" she said, and they both spent the next few minutes laughing.

Felicity's family remained attentive throughout the two weeks. The novelty of having a daughter and sister home again after so long did not easily wear thin. She was taken visiting everywhere, shown off proudly to old acquaintances and new. She sat in the cushioned pew with the rest of the family during the Sunday-morning service at church, bowing and smiling at familiar faces, some of them grown-up and married since she had last known them with any degree of intimacy.

Mr. Moorehead delivered the sermon. He was an earnest young man, tall and slender, with a shock of unruly blond hair that did not quite suit the image of sobriety that he went to great pains to project. He had a fair complexion that had an unfortunate tendency to flush easily. It did just that on several occasions when his eyes strayed to their pew where the twins were sitting, pert and pretty. It is true, Felicity thought with amusement. He does like them. She was not so sure, though, that he could not tell them apart. His eyes more often rested on the twin sitting next to her than on the one sitting farther along the seat between Mama and Papa. Laura! After a couple of days at home, Felicity had finally sorted out which was which. Although indistinguishable as far as physical traits were concerned, there was a slight difference in nature. Both were exuberant, talkative, and giggly, but Laura was a trifle more serious and kindhearted than her twin. Lucy had a little more mischief and sparkle. And it was Laura Mr. Moorehead fancied. When they left the church, he stood on the steps outside, looking youthful and handsome in his surplice, shaking the hands of the parishioners. There was no way he could have kept his eyes on the twins all the way from their pew, Felicity decided, and the girls were dressed identically, even down to the yellow ribbons that tied their bonnets beneath the chin. But still, he shook hands politely with Lucy and flushed quite noticeably when it came to Laura's turn. Felicity smiled, placed her hand in his, and complimented him on the thoughtfulness of his sermon.

The twins allowed a week to pass before they put into effect their plan. They exercised unusual restraint, realizing that they would stand a better chance of success if they gave their sister time to get to know them, time to become really fond of them again. The love and attention they lavished on her was by no means hypocritical, but all the same they watched and gauged her mood.

Their chance finally came one morning when Felicity invited them to her room to show them some of her fans, jewels, shawls, and other delights. It was raining outside, but not an unpleasant, misty, cold rain that would have sent all their spirits plummeting. This was a steady, windless downpour that anyone could see would clear up before noon, leaving the sky blue again and the grass and flower petals twinkling with moisture.

"Did this really come all the way from Paris?" Lucy sighed as she spread an ivory fan in her lap and examined the bird that was brightly painted on its surface.

"And these are the gloves you wore when you were presented to the queen," Laura stated. She did not need to ask. They had both been told the astonishing fact on a previous occasion. "The Prince Regent actually touched them, Felicity, when he led you into the dance."

"Yes, indeed," her sister replied.

"What is he like?" Lucy asked eagerly. "Adrian saw him once driving past in a procession on the street. He said the prince is enormously fat and has a preposterous cluster of curls at the front of his head that look for all the world as if they are about to tumble down over his nose."

"Oh, dear," Felicity said with a laugh. "Yes, I cannot deny that he is a mountain of a man. But he has great charm and ease of manner. When he asked me to dance, I felt that I had two left feet, ten thumbs, and a brain full of feathers. But within minutes he had me talking and laughing and feeling for all the world as though I were dancing with any ordinary mortal."

"How wonderful it must be to see him and the queen, and to mix with the *ton* and have all these beautiful things," Lucy said with a sigh, and she caught her twin's eye quite by accident. But a message passed. Now is the time, they seemed to say to each other. If we do not ask now, the opportunity may be lost forever.

"Felicity," Laura said. Days before it had been decided that she would be the spokeswoman. "Do you think it would be possible, I mean if you would not mind terribly, and if Mama and Papa could be induced to consent. I am quite sure they would if *you* were to ask them. And we would promise to be ever so good and to pay heed to you and allow you to teach us what is right and what is expected. Just for this one year, you see. We do not ask for more, and indeed it would be more than Maude or Harriet or any of our other friends can expect in a lifetime. And we would be forever grateful, would we not, Lucy?"

"What on earth are you trying to say, love?" Felicity asked, interrupting this muddled monologue and her task of arranging fan and gloves and other items in the box where they were stored.

"Will you take us to London with you for the Season?" Lucy blurted, leaping to her feet and forgetting that her twin had been appointed the one with the greater tact and the one more likely to get what they wanted.

Felicity stopped immediately what she was doing and looked from one to the other of her sisters. "To London?" she repeated. "You mean this year? Next week?"

"Yes!" Lucy cried. "We are eighteen already, Felicity, closer to nineteen, in fact. And we shall never have a chance of a Season unless you take us. Mama has said that Papa just does not have money enough to take us. But he does have some money, Felicity. I am sure he would give us a generous allowance for clothes and pin money. You would be able to provide us with a home and food," she added naively.

"We have always dreamed of going to London," Laura added, "ever since you came home last, Felicity, and looked so fine in your gowns and town carriage. But we never expected it to be reality. We would not have dreamed of asking you if Sir Wilfred were still alive, because then we would have been asking for his hospitality and it would not have seemed right. But you are our sister, so we do not feel it is wrong to ask."

"Oh, please, Felicity," Lucy begged, seating herself on the high bed and looking at her sister with anxious eyes.

Felicity looked from one to the other again. "What does Mama say about this?" she asked.

"Oh!" wailed Laura. "We have not mentioned it to her. She would surely have forbidden us to bother you with such a request. But I am sure she will agree if the suggestion seems to come from you, Felicity. She is enormously proud of you, you know. I do not believe you can do anything wrong in her eyes."

Felicity resumed her task of packing the box. She desperately needed time to think, yet the twins were sitting there, leaning forward in their eagerness, waiting for her decision. She did not know why she had not thought of it herself. It was a perfectly splendid idea. It was only right that her sisters be given the chance of a Season in London, the chance to find themselves suitable husbands, and of course the expense to herself would be no burden at all. She had money, and to spare. And even if she not not, she would have been willing to economize for the sake of her family.

And having the twins with her in London would be quite delightful. They would be company for her at home. And no one could possibly deplore her own lone state when it became evident that *she* was the chaperone, supervising her sisters' come-out. She would be able to give a ball for them in Wilfred's—her—home on Pall Mall. The house boasted a perfectly magnificent ballroom that she had not really planned to use this year. But now. . . .

She looked up and smiled sparklingly at a tense

set of twins. "Why did I not think of this myself?" she said. "I shall go talk to Mama immediately."

The twins squealed loudly and rushed at her. "She is in the morning room writing to Adrian," Laura said. "Let us go right away."

Felicity laughed and held up a hand. "No," she said, "I said I would talk to Mama. If you two went to her in your present mood, she would more likely pack you off to the schoolroom for another year of lessons than to London for the Season."

It was not difficult to persuade Mrs. Maynard to agree to the scheme, especially as Felicity made it sound as if the idea had been entirely her own. She worried about the expense, she worried that the twins would be a burden to their sister, but she was not unaware of the great opportunity that was being offered her younger girls.

Mr. Maynard was a little more difficult to persuade. He had accepted money from Felicity in the past, or at least from her husband when she married. He had used that money wisely and made himself and those dependent upon him secure. He did not wish to be beholden to his daughter again. However, when she assured him that her household expenses would hardly be increased by the girls' presence and that he could keep them in pin money, he weakened. He finally capitulated when she clasped her arms around his neck, sat on his lap as she had used to do a great deal as a girl, and assured him that he would be doing her a great favor if he could spare the twins for a few months. She had been *so* lonely since Wilfred died. And who better to keep her company than her own sisters?

The tempo of life increased to near-fever pitch for the remaining week of Felicity's stay at home. Trunks had to be found for each of the twins and those trunks had to be filled. They had absolutely nothing to wear; their hair was an absolute mess; they had completely forgotten how to dance, and so on and on. Felicity endured it all with the greatest good nature, assuring them that there was no need to beg the village dressmaker to sit up night and day for the next week sewing for them. She would take them to her own dressmaker as soon as they arrived in London. Yes, the clothing money that Papa had allotted would be quite sufficient to cover all their needs. She refrained from admitting that in fact the money was unlikely to pay for even a tenth of all that the girls would need. She promised the girls that her own hairdresser would be summoned to the house the moment of their arrival so that they might face the London world with fashionable heads. And a dancing master would be summoned long before they were to attend their first ball, so that they might brush up on all their steps, and even learn to waltz.

Tom was pounced upon as soon as he entered the house on the day the decision was made. He had walked across during the afternoon as soon as the rain stopped and the clouds moved away from the sun. By the time he arrived in the sitting room, a good-natured grin on his face, he had a twin hanging from each arm.

"You will go down in history as a public benefactress, Flick," he said after greeting Mrs. Maynard. "I hear you are going to rid the neighborhood of these two little brats for a few months."

They both cried out in protest and dropped his arms.

"Do you think your constitution is strong enough to stand it?" he continued, still grinning at Felicity.

"Oh, horrid!" Lucy cried. "If you feel such pity for her, sir, why do you not come to London, too? You could help her keep an eye on us."

"I decided a long time ago," Tom lied with a smile, "that I would spend some time in town this spring. Even we rustics feel the need to have the cobwebs blown off us occasionally, you know. But knowing that you two are to be there on the loose might very well cause me to change my mind."

"Tom?" Felicity was smiling radiantly at him. "You are coming to London, too? For the Season? Oh, how perfectly delightful this spring is going to be. My sisters and my dearest friend and London and the Season all together!"

4

It was a very gay entourage that traveled to London the following week. There had been much talk and laughter—and some tears—as the girls bade their parents farewell. But finally Felicity's coach was on the way, the twins almost immediately forgetting the sadness of waving good-bye to Mama and Papa and exclaiming over the soft opulence of the velvet seats and the efficiency of the springs.

Lucy bounced up and down in her seat a few times. "Indeed, Felicity," she said, "if it were not for the swaying of the vehicle, I would not know that we were in a carriage. This is heavenly."

"Yes," Laura added, "one feels thoroughly jounced around in Papa's carriage just during the short ride to church."

Tom rode alongside them. He had intended to travel separately, a few days later, but the persuasions of the twins and the eager smiles of Felicity had caused him to change his mind. He had sent his baggage on a day ahead and agreed to accompany the ladies.

"Though if you have the idea that I shall be able to protect you on the way," he had said, "you may be sadly disappointed. If I saw a footpad or highwayman about to attack you, I should probably turn tail and run, you know."

The twins had giggled. "No, you would not, Mr.

Russell," Laura had assured him. "You would put up your fists and defend us to the death even if they came at us with blunderbusses. I know you would."

"Yes, I have to agree, Tom," Felicity had said. "I always used to think that I would prefer to face someone else's cudgel than your fists."

Tom rode along beside the carriage, occasionally giving his horse its head and cantering on for a few miles. The day was perfect for a journey, cloudy and cool, but neither windy nor wet. Yet he wondered as the landmarks of home gradually disappeared behind him what the devil he was doing. He had had no intention of visiting London this year, let alone spending the Season there and participating in all its social events. He despised such activities. For him they spelled utter boredom. The thought of going had leapt into his mind only when Lucy had asked why he would not. And he had said quite steadily, without a moment's hesitation, that for a long time he had been planning to go. What had possessed him?

And why now? He could quite easily have made excuses for postponing his departure. He could have gone up later just for a couple of weeks, maybe. All sorts of arrangements had had to be made for leaving his home and his lands for a few months. But, no, here he was on his way, all the arrangements having been made at a frantic pace in the last week. He must be mad.

Or just in love! Tom had known fully before she returned that he loved Felicity and would always do so. But he had thought that his love had matured and mellowed. He had not thought of himself as being *in* love. Not until he saw her again, that was. The sun had brightened her hair and the wind had gently rustled her gown as he had approached her on the lawn. She had looked like a half-forgotten dream, not real at all. He had kept his eyes off her as he got nearer, concentrating on the flowers, the blue sky, her mother. And then, when he had finally turned, he had known, even as he held his hand out

to her and spoke calmly. Calmly, that is, except that
he had not called her Lady Wren as he had planned
to do, or even Felicity, but quite unintentionally by
the name that he had always used for her since she
was six years old. He had known then, as his eyes
took in her mature beauty, her expensive clothes,
and her radiant smile, that his case was utterly hopeless. He was as much in love with her as he had ever
been; he was like a schoolboy with thumping heart-
beat and pounding temples. He had forgotten everything for a moment when she had come quite
unexpectedly into his arms. He would have kissed
her right there on the lawn, with her mother standing not three yards away, had he not suddenly noticed, with something of a shock, that there was no
answering passion in her eyes, only a very bright
friendliness. He had laughed instead and turned the
moment into a joke.

It had taken a great deal of self-discipline during
those two weeks to quell the aroused passions that
seeing her again had created. He had known it, of
course. He had known that she could no longer love
him, that time and distance would have taken her
far beyond him. He had hoped that they would still
be friendly acquaintances. But it hurt, nonetheless,
when she talked with such freedom and such enthusiasm about her plans for the future. He knew that
his deepest hopes could never be realized when she
talked to him so openly about the type of man she
planned to take for her second husband. And it was
true that she had moved far from him. She had
become part of that sophisticated society in which he
felt so ill-at-ease, reveling in enjoyment for enjoyment's sake, setting no store whatsoever on love
and sober contentment.

But mingled with disappointment was a great elation over the fact that they were to remain friends—
very close friends, in fact. Felicity had seemed able
to resume their closeness, without the passion, with
the greatest of ease. It was as if she had forgotten

that there had ever been anything else in their relationship. And he was willing to accept her on her own terms. It was not that Tom was grasping at straws, willing to take any part of her that was offered. Rather, he really loved her, not with the selfish need for gratification that pure sexual passion often brings, but with the selflessness of true love. If she wanted his friendship, she should have it. If she needed him as a confidant, then he would always be there for her.

Perhaps this was the reason why he had made the very irrational decision to go to London. Felicity would be alone there, searching for her dream. A friend needed to be close. If he were there with her, perhaps he would be able to add some stability to her life. He could be her escort when she lacked one, her friend when she needed one. And he would be able to see her, talk to her, be with her, until she found another man to marry. When that happened, Tom would return to the country, to the quiet life that he had resigned himself to.

It was a mad scheme, Tom thought ruefully as he pulled back on his horse's reins and eased it into a walk to allow the carriage to come up with him again. It was one that was bound to bring him much unnecessary heartache, and it might take him many months again once he reached home to restore the tranquillity of mind that had been so hard to achieve the first time. But he could not do otherwise. Those twins might prove to be more of a handful than she expected. They might need the support of a man who was always available.

Inside the carriage all was gaiety—or almost all. Lucy, alone on one seat, continually slid back and forth, fearful that while she was gazing eagerly from one window she was missing something on the other side. Felicity gave up trying to convince her sister that until they came to the next town or the next tollgate, all that was to be seen was fields and more fields.

"And the grass grows green twenty miles from home just as it does on Papa's land," she pointed out.

"Oh, what is London like?" the girl asked. "Will we see it from a great way off, Felicity?"

"Yes, we will," she replied, "but not for many hours yet, love. You might just as well sit still and reserve your energy for exploring the house on Pall Mall this evening."

Laura too was eager. She sat forward whenever they approached a village or town, watched with interested eyes the great novelty of a different inn and church and blacksmith's forge from the ones with which they were long familiar. Between towns, though, she sat in relative quiet, her chin resting on her hand, gazing absently at the passing fields.

Felicity watched her occasionally with a thoughtful expression. She wondered with a mixture of amusement and genuine concern if Mr. Moorehead had anything to do with the girl's preoccupation. Two days ago, on Sunday, she had made the same observations as she had the week before. The curate could definitely tell the twins apart, and he most certainly had a preference for Laura. Lucy had mentioned to him on the way out of church that she and her twin would be going to London for the Season. He had flushed even more than he had the previous week when it came Laura's turn to shake his hand.

And then just the day before, Felicity and her sisters had driven into the village to make some last-minute purchases. They had been coming out of the haberdasher's shop when they had walked almost literally into the curate on the street. Mr. Moorehead had raised his hat and exchanged a few pleasantries, and Felicity and Lucy had walked on. It was several minutes before Felicity realized that Laura was not with them. When she glanced back, it was to see her sister smiling prettily up at the curate, whose face, for once, was not flushed. Felicity and

Lucy stood for several minutes, gazing into the harness maker's window, before their sister joined them.

"I wonder if Mr. Moorehead knows which twin decided to be polite and linger to talk with him?" Lucy had said with a giggle.

Laura giggled too. "I wonder," she agreed.

But thinking about it now as she watched her sister gaze sightlessly from the carriage window, Felicity was almost certain that Laura knew very well that Mr. Moorehead could distinguish her from her twin and that he had a *tendre* for her. How did Laura feel toward him? Felicity wondered. Her absentmindedness now suggested an interest. Well, she thought, if Laura was interested in the young man, it was a very good thing that she was going to have a Season. Under her guidance, Laura would meet many young men and would find out that life had a great deal more excitement to offer than the life of a parson's wife. After all, look what would have happened to her if Wilfred had not decided to visit a friend in Sussex when he had. She would be married to Tom.

The object of that thought drew level with the window of the coach at that moment, and with a bright smile Felicity leaned forward. "Tom, you have been ahead of us for a long time," she said. "Have you slain many highwaymen?"

"No, no," he replied, "merely cracked a few jaws. Shall we stop at the next inn for luncheon?"

"I am positively starved," Lucy announced, and Laura giggled.

The *beau monde* was not unaware of the fact that Sir Wilfred Wren's widow was returning to town. The news spread very quickly via the downstairs route, as much news did in the city, filtering upstairs gradually as it moved from house to house. One of the kitchen maids in the Wren household had told her young man, a footman in another house, who had told his brother, an undergroom in a third house, who had told his drinking friend, a junior chef in a fourth house, and so on, that instructions had been received to prepare the house for occupancy.

Lady Wren had always drawn eyes like a magnet. Many could remember her as she had been as a young bride: shy and a little eager, often clinging to the arm of old Wren. Others remembered her only as she had become in more recent years: proud, aloof, mysteriously unknown, and always close to her husband. All remembered her almost flawless beauty, the glorious thick, golden hair, the poised, shapely body, the half-smile that often curved her lips, the rather dreamy eyes—bedroom eyes, Lord Edmond Waite had once called them.

But none of her former acquaintances could quite imagine the widow without her aged watchdog of a husband. One of the mysteries surrounding her had always been the question of whether she had stayed close to Wren purely from choice or whether he had been an old tyrant and very strict with her. Certainly it had been expected that she would take a lover within a year or two of her marriage. Old Wren could not have had much to offer in the way of sexual excitement, after all. Yet there was never a breath of scandal involving her name. Either she was a faithful wife or she conducted her affairs with unusual discretion. Most subscribed to the latter theory. One had only to look at Lady Wren, at her physical beauty and that sensual look on her face, to know that she was a woman of passion and experience. Many concluded that her amours must have been conducted on the Continent, where she would be less likely to incur malicious gossip.

But many wondered what she would be like now, a young, beautiful, and extremely wealthy widow. Surely some of the reserve would be lowered. Surely now she would be inclined to participate fully in the pleasures of life among the *ton*. Many waited eagerly for their first glimpse of her.

They were to have their opportunity on an eve-

ning two days after the arrival of Felicity and her
party in London. It had been difficult to restrain the
twins even that long. They were ready to rush out
and conquer the world the morning after their arrival, and they were quite downhearted to discover
that the whole of the day was to be spent at home.
Excitement grew, though, when a dressmaker arrived and footmen spent a whole ten minutes carrying in bolts of fabric and various accessories. Patterns
were chosen and fabrics and trimmings; measure-
ments were taken; and before the twins had time to
be bored, the morning was over, and the dressmaker had promised to have one evening gown apiece
for the three ladies made and delivered by the following day. Much of the afternoon was taken up
with the delight of having their hair styled. Both
twins were enchanted by their close-cropped dark
curls with longer ringlets that had been allowed to
trail down their necks.

Tom had come for dinner and was able to tell
them that after a night spent at Pulteney's Hotel he
had been able to find suitable rooms for himself. He
had given this information when allowed to get a
word in edgewise between lengthy spells of hearing
all about the dressmaker and hairdresser.

Felicity had chosen the theater as a suitable setting
for her first appearance since Wilfred's death and for
the introduction of her sisters to the eyes of the *ton*.
They would not, of course, attend any balls or major
social functions until their official come-out. She had
set the wheels in motion already for a grand ball to
be held in her own home the following week.

Tom accompanied them to the theater. Felicity
gazed at him fondly when he was announced. He
really looked quite handsome in his dark-blue velvet
evening coat and paler-blue knee breeches, though
she was sure that many of the men of fashion would
view with some contempt the simplicity of the folds
of his neckcloth and his absence of all ornaments.
He looked very dear, nonetheless, and in her ner-

vousness at meeting society for the first time without Wilfred, she would not have exchanged him for the most exquisite dandy of them all. She smiled and held out her hands to him.

"Tom, how splendid you look," she said. "Will you mind if I cling tightly to your arm tonight? I feel almost nervous."

"You, Flick?" he said, taking her hands and squeezing them reassuringly. "You will be the most beautiful lady there tonight. There is no doubt in my mind."

"Flatterer!" she said, grinning wickedly at him. "And you must not say any such thing in the presence of my sisters. They are still upstairs before their looking glasses, made speechless by their own splendor."

"Any chance it will last?" Tom asked. "The speechlessness, I mean."

The theater was almost full when they entered the box that had once belonged to Sir Wilfred Wren. Felicity had not meant to make such a seemingly calculated entrance, but the twins had caused several delays, first being late to come downstairs, then having to rush back up several times to retrieve forgotten items. They had got as far as the carriage when Laura remembered, with a shriek, that she did not have with her the fan that she had spent all of half an hour choosing that morning.

Felicity found that her old public manner returned to her on this occasion almost like second nature. She was aware of many eyes on her as she stepped first into the box. She did not think she imagined a heightened murmur of voices as the twins entered after her. But she waited calmly, lips curved in a smile, dreamy eyes resting on the stage, until Tom came up behind her and arranged her chair. She sat down, rested one arm negligently on the velvet-coverd edge of the box, and turned to talk to her companions. She had not directly looked at anyone else in the theater.

Laura and Lucy felt no such shyness. Their eager, dancing eyes went everywhere: from the pit crowded with young bucks to the tiers of boxes crowded with ladies and gentlemen decked in unimagined finery.

"Felicity," Laura hissed, "everyone is *looking* at us."

"Is it not considered rude," Lucy added, "for so many gentlemen to be gazing this way through quizzing glasses?"

"You will have to forgive them all on this one occasion," Tom said with a grin. "They must all be wondering if they drank one too many glasses of port with their dinners that they are seeing double."

The twins giggled.

"And you are both looking so outstandingly pretty," Felicity added, "that they must be hoping they are not."

Indeed, the twins were receiving their fair share of attention. There were more new debutantes to be gazed upon every day, and many of them were pretty, but no others came in pairs. No one seemed to know who they were or what their connection with Lady Wren was, but the question was definitely worth investigating.

The twins might have been chagrined, though, had they known that most of the attention directed on their box was focused on their sister. She was as beautiful and as enigmatic as ever, everyone noticed. She looked quite ravishing in a gown of shimmering silver satin, low in the bodice, high in the waist, exquisitely but simply designed. Sapphires sparkled at her neck and ears and on the hand that lay on the edge of the box. Her head, with its masses of golden hair, rested almost arrogantly on a proudly arched neck. She appeared as remote and unattainable as she ever had when Sir Wilfred Wren had been her constant shadow.

Many of the gentlemen present eyed her either openly or surreptitiously. She had much to make her attractive. Her beauty alone would have ensured her

admirers enough. Her wealth made her irresistible
to those—and there were many—whose exquisite
dress and languid, courtly manners belied the fact
that their pockets were sadly to let and that they
were on the lookout for a rich wife. If that wife
should also be beautiful, they could not ask for more
of life.

Several fashionable ladies were no less interested
in viewing the widow. She showed no signs of having suffered from her recent bereavement. She had
clearly returned to the capital husband-hunting and
was making a shocking display of her wealth. The
sapphire necklace alone surely made a loud-enough
statement. Did she really need the earrings and ring
as well? She was behaving in a proper-enough manner, they were forced to concede. She was on display, but she was not ogling any of the men. Well,
good luck to her. She had endured the attentions of
a doddering old man for long enough. Perhaps she
deserved now to reap the rewards. Several of these
ladies gazed curiously at the twins who shared her
box, and more intently at her male companion. Most
could not remember seeing him before, and dismissed him as an object not worthy of greater attention. The lorgnettes moved on to other new arrivals.

Lord Edmond Waite, occupying his own box with
his intended, Lady Dorothea Page, and her brother
and sister-in-law, eyed the widow through narrowed
pale-blue eyes. His long, aristocratic face, with its
aquiline nose and thin lips, was expressionless. He
allowed the shallow conversation of his companions
to wash over him as he toyed with the handle of his
quizzing glass. He did not raise it to his eye.

She was as desirable as ever—perhaps more so.
She was the sort of woman who improved with age.
Her curves seemed more pronounced, her face more
full of character than had been the case six years
before when he had first made a proposition to her.
He had been surprised and a little piqued by her
refusal on that occasion. He could not, after all,

imagine that that old man of a husband was capable of giving her much in the way of satisfaction in bed. And she was surely a woman of unusual passion. Every movement of her body proclaimed the fact, even if one ignored those incredible bedroom eyes. He had concluded at the time that she must be afraid of her husband, who was always close to her. It would have been difficult for one so young to develop the duplicity to get away from him often enough to conduct a satisfactory *affaire de coeur*.

But Lord Waite had never abandoned the idea of one day possessing her as a mistress. Making her his wife was, of course, out of the question. The alliance between his family and Dorothea's had been planned since her infancy, and the formal betrothal must be made soon, he supposed. He would find it difficult to avoid such a conclusion. But, anyway, he had no desire to wed the widow. Even though she possessed such remarkable beauty and such enormous wealth, she was really a little nobody who had had the good sense to snare that old fool for a husband, or whose parents had had the good sense. No, Dorothea would suit him very well as a bride. She was an aristocratic iceberg who would be quite contented to ignore his extramarital adventures, provided he bred his heirs on her. And Waite could not picture himself remaining interested in one woman for very long once he had possessed her, not even the delectable widow.

But he had to have her. Across the width of the theater he slowly undressed her with his eyes and felt the heat of desire stirring in him. He did not anticipate any opposition. Women almost always succumbed to him. He did not even have to stray from his own class to find willing bedfellows. He was very tall and a trifle too thin, in his own estimation, but he had an athletic physique that made him powerfully attractive. Although he knew that his face was not handsome, he knew too that women seemed to find its very harshness intriguing. The widow would be his soon, and indeed the delay had been a long one.

Lord Waite spared one measured glance for the twin girls, who were much too young for his taste, and for the man who shared their box, but he dismissed the latter as a quite unimportant obstacle. Finally he gave his attention to something his intended was saying.

Felicity, during the drive home, judged the evening to have been a great success. A good number of her acquaintances, most of them influential, had visited her box during the intervals between acts. Now that it had been seen publicly that she was in residence again and out of mourning, the invitations would begin to arrive. And now that the twins had been seen, the *beau monde* was bound to flock to her ball the coming week to become further acquainted with the unusual spectacle of twin debutantes, as alike as peas in a pod.

The twins giggled and bubbled with the excitement of it all.

The play had been quite good, too, Tom added.

5

The pace of life certainly picked up after that visit to the theater. Even the next day, cards were left in the visitors' tray, invitations arrived, and visitors were admitted. Felicity reestablished contact with many of her husband's old friends, most of them in the middle or later stages of life. The twins were introduced to many people. They were allowed to accompany their sister to a smallish gathering for the birthday of Sir Humphrey Browne, and to a musical evening presented by Mrs. Hornsby. They made numerous excursions to the shops, where they purchased necessary and unnecessary accessories for their new wardrobes. And they drove in the park several afternoons with Felicity in her landau, escorted by Tom.

They were seen and admired. The activities were enough to intrigue the *ton*, who soon discovered that the girls were the sisters of Lady Wren. The challenge of getting to know them and learning to distinguish one from the other was enough to make Lady Wren's ball the most popular social event of the Season so far. The added fascination of seeing the widow herself at a ball, alone for the first time in memory, was enough to ensure a perfect squeeze of a crowd. Everyone wanted to see how she would behave. Would she keep herself as aloof from others as she always had, or would she begin to show favors to another man? And if so, which man? Many a hopeful gallant dressed himself with particular care for the evening's entertainment. It would be the coup of the Season to be the acknowledged favorite of Lady Wren.

The twins were wild with excitement. Felicity had decided not to entertain for dinner. Thus, as soon as the meal was over, an hour earlier than usual, they were all at liberty to retire to their rooms to get ready. Felicity had hidden her own high spirits behind a facade of amusement. But she was excited and extremely nervous, she admitted when she was alone in her room with her maid. So much depended upon the next few hours. First of all, of course, there was the responsibility of handling the twins' comeout. It was so important that they make a good first impression. They had little more than beauty and youthful high spirits to recommend them. Papa was no longer poor, but neither was he in a position to offer large dowries with the girls. Felicity could have done so, but would not wound her father's pride by suggesting such a thing. Anyway, she reasoned, it was perhaps better so. Any man who showed interest in the girls would be likely to do so for honorable reasons. And she hoped beyond anything that her sisters would find suitable husbands during the next few months. She did not think that Papa would agree to their coming another year, and what type of husbands could be found in the country? Only dull stay-at-homes who would destroy the exuberance of the girls in no time at all.

But Felicity was not really afraid for the twins. They were extremely pretty, she knew, even discounting a sister's partiality, and they had the sort of high spirits that would set them above the ordinary. They were well-behaved girls and could be trusted to act as they ought tonight. No, it was for herself that she felt her heart thump and her stomach churn. She wanted to attract. She wanted to dissociate herself from the older segments of society. Yet she did not wish to appear wild or to attract the wrong sort of man. Truth to tell, she did not know how to behave. When she had first come to town as Wilfred's bride, she had been overwhelmed with shyness. She had not been introduced gradually into the *ton* as a debutante. She had been hurled into the middle of it as the wife of a fairly prominent member of society. She had immediately and quite unconsciously retreated behind a mask of aloofness. Quite without realizing what she was doing, she had always, when facing company, straightened her spine, thrown back her shoulders, raised her chin, and faced those people with slightly drooped eyelids and half-smiling lips. No one, not even Wilfred, she thought, knew that behind the facade was a slightly frightened girl who ached with eagerness to mix freely with those grand and glittering people, but who did not know quite how it was to be done. So she had hovered close to Wilfred as the only safe anchor in her new world, smiled at people, rarely talked, and repulsed any improper advances with disdainful manner and wildly beating heart.

Felicity was old enough now and had been part of the social scene long enough to have analyzed herself. She knew that she had a reputation for poise and cool sophistication. She knew equally that that was not her at all. No one really knew her, except perhaps her family and Tom. And she did not want to shatter the image. It had proved useful. It was something to hide behind. Yet she must unbend enough to be approachable. She did not wish to risk a lonely Season in which she would be viewed as the aloof widow whose sole function this year was to introduce her sisters to the *ton*. She wanted to enjoy life. She wanted the events of the evening to set her on the path to a dazzling future. But she must watch for fortune-hunters. She was well aware that her wealth would attract many men for all the wrong reasons. Fortunately, she had been in town enough times to know the men most likely to be

after her money. They would very often be the ones
most elegantly dressed, most apparently bored with
all the splendor surrounding them. They would be
the ones who spent their nights gambling, their days
spending money they did not have. They would be
the ones gentlemanly enough to dance with the
plainest girls, if those girls had wealthy papas.

Felicity had unconsciously chosen a gown that
enhanced her image. It was of shimmering gold satin
and fell in generous folds from its high waistline,
gleaming with every move she made. It was completely unadorned, its neckline low, its short sleeves
puffed. She wore with it white lace gloves and Wilfred's emeralds. Her hair, piled into a smooth chignon, with curled tendrils at her neck and temple,
was bare of the plumes that most matrons and many
of the younger women would wear.

She looked at herself in a full-length mirror as the
maid clasped the emeralds at the back of her neck.
"Well, will I do?" she asked, tapping her ivory fan
against the palm of one hand.

"I never saw you look lovelier, ma'am," the girl
replied, a look of genuine admiration in her eyes.

Felicity smiled and left the room to pay a visit on
her sisters. They shared a dressing room between
their separate bedrooms. It seemed safe to go there
rather than down into the drawing room. In the
short while since she had become reacquainted with
them, Felicity had learned that punctuality was not
one of her sisters' virtues. They were still there, all
ready except that Lucy was missing a slipper.

"I know it is here somewhere," she was saying,
exasperated. "I carried them in here in the box.
Come on, Laura, let's look again. Oh, Felicity, how
simply gorgeous you look. You will quite put us in
the shade."

"Hardly," Felicity said, stooping down and picking up the offending slipper from beneath a dis-
carded petticoat. "You two have youth and vitality
on your side. And you both look extremely lovely."

She stood back to examine their appearance. They both wore delicate white lace overdresses of silk. Both had long white gloves, pearl necklaces, ribbons threaded through their dark curls, and silk fans. They looked almost totally identical. But it had seemed a wicked trick to play on the *ton* to make it well nigh impossible to tell the difference between them. Laura's underdress was the palest yellow; Lucy's, green.

"Now, when we are in the receiving line, I shall have to remember to tell everyone to repeat after me," Felicity said, " 'Miss Lucy Maynard, green; Miss Laura Maynard, yellow.' "

The twins giggled. "Do you really think many people will come?" Laura asked anxiously.

"If everyone who answered the invitations puts in an appearance, I do not quite know where we are to put them all," Felicity replied.

Two hours later Felicity dared to judge her ball a success. She and the twins had stood in the receiving line for upward of an hour shaking hands, smiling, accepting compliments, laughing at good humored jokes about the likeness of the girls. And almost as soon as they left the line to join their guests in the ballroom, their cards had rapidly filled up so that almost all they had to do for the rest of the evening was relax and enjoy themselves and wait for the next partner to come and claim them.

The twins were going to be a success, Felicity could see. She had made sure in the last week and a half that they had all the clothes they would need, that they had fashionable hairstyles, that they practiced their dancing steps under the instruction of a dancing master. They had even learned the waltz, though it was likely to be a few weeks before they would be granted permission to dance it in public. But she had not instructed them in how they would be expected to behave in society. She found their manners delightful, and she knew from personal experience that Mama's teaching through their childhood and girlhood had been quite thorough. She refused to tell them that debutantes were expected to behave as if they had been on the town for years, with a sort of languid boredom that would hide their naiveté. Let the twins enjoy themselves. Let them laugh if they were delighted, talk nonstop if they wished to communicate, and sparkle with exuberance if they felt so inclined.

Thus, while many of the younger women around them fanned themselves languidly, complained of the heat and the squeeze, and smiled with weary resignation at the men who came to partner them, Lucy and Laura laughed and smiled, talked eagerly to their partners, gazed admiringly at the blazing chandeliers and the lavish floral arrangements, and quickly gathered about themselves a veritable court of young bucks, eager to claim their attention between dances, offering to bring them lemonade, and trying, by looking only at their faces, to tell which was which. This game gave rise to several explosions of giggles and guffaws that brought quizzing glasses and lorgnettes swiveling in their direction.

Felicity was delighted to see that the girls had attracted partners of all ranks. The poker-faced son of the Duke of Cheswick danced with each of them in turn and was actually seen to smile—a very rare occurrence—at Lucy once. The Earl of Darlington danced with Lucy, Viscount Varley with Laura. And there was a whole host of gentlemen of lower rank. Yes, she decided, she really did not have to worry about her sisters.

She was encouraged on her own account, too. She had opened the ball with Tom and had been most grateful for his warm, steady hand and his dear, familiar face. He was giving her that eyes-only smile, she had noticed, and had felt instantly at her ease. She had been able to smile genuinely at him and talk without constraint. He had helped her remove the old mask that she had kept firmly in place when in the receiving line. At the end of the dance, Tom had scribbled his name in her empty card for a waltz after the supper hour. And he had moved away to allow others to come and pay their respects and fill up her card before the next dance began.

Ever since that time she had danced, several times with older acquaintances of her husband, but sometimes, too, with younger, more eligible men. She had tried her best to relax, to talk to them as she had talked to Tom, to smile directly into their eyes instead of retreating behind the half-smile and the drooped eyelids. It was reassuring to find Tom at her elbow on several occasions between dances, ready to talk good-naturedly about the success of the ball. He danced every dance, Felicity noticed, usually with the plainer girls, whose mamas or chaperones were not making enough of an effort to find them partners. Always he was smiling at them, and always talking, so that he drew answering smiles from even the shiest and most downhearted. Dear Tom! How fortunate would be the girl who finally snared him for a husband. She did not for a moment believe his claim that he was confirmed in his bachelorhood.

Lord Edmond Waite claimed the supper dance, a waltz. Felicity had been a little alarmed at the end of the first set when he had bowed before her, looked at her penetratingly with his pale-blue eyes, and signed his name in bold letters next to that particular dance. He had not said a word—someone else was talking to her at the time—but had merely bowed again and walked away. Felicity had felt herself breathless for a few moments afterward. That particular man had always made her feel a little afraid, though she was not at all sure why. His appearance was certainly compelling. She would not call him handsome. There was nothing perfect about either his face or his physique. Yet he was the sort of man who somehow drew one's attention. Was it the proud, arrogant bearing of the man? Was it the way he dressed, always elegantly and expensively, yet with none of the extremes of fashion of the dandy? Or was it his eyes, which seemed able to see right through a person's clothing, right through a person's eyes to the very soul? He was certainly looking remarkably splendid this evening, dressed entirely in blue satin to match his eyes and white silk stockings and linen.

And Felicity remembered, as she always did whenever she saw him, how at a party in honor of his mother's remarriage, many years before, he had sat down beside her and talked for a long while, mesmerizing her with those eyes, and had finally asked her, just as if he were inquiring if she would like another cup of tea, if she would come upstairs with him to his bed. Her aloof mask had completely hidden her shock. She had managed a cool, even icy refusal. But ever since, his eyes had seemed to mock her whenever she accidentally met them.

And now she was dancing with him, for the first time ever, and a waltz at that, the most intimate of dances. She looked hastily around to assure herself that Lucy and Laura were sitting out with their partners, as was proper during the waltz, and returned her attention to her own partner, whose well-manicured hand and satin-clad shoulder she trembled to touch. She retreated instantly behind her mask.

"Well, Felicity," he said, "how does it feel to be free of your watchdog at last?"

The mask did not serve her. She looked up at him in shock. "Are you referring to my husband, my lord?" she asked.

He laughed. "I have noticed, ma'am, in the course of the evening," he said, "that you are quite capable of opening those lovely eyes quite wide and of smiling enough to show your quite perfect teeth. I was not going to have you freeze up on me."

She continued to look at him, not sure whether to smile or to stand back and smack his face. His words had been calculatedly insolent. Felicity, indeed! And watchdog, indeed.

He laughed again. "So which is it to be?" he asked as if he had read her thoughts. "Are you going to allow your sense of the absurd to win and laugh, or am I about to have my feet stamped on? I do assure you, ma'am, that your ball will go down as the sensation of the Season if you do the latter. I believe many eyes are on us."

Felicity allowed herself to relax and said nothing.

"You must have remarkably handsome parents," Lord Waite continued, "if they have been able to produce three such extraordinarily beautiful daughters. I congratulate you on the success of your sisters. But I hope, ma'am, that their appearance will not relegate you to the position of chaperone merely?" It was a question.

Felicity smiled. "I fully intend to gain enjoyment from the Season, too, my lord," she said, and she realized only as the words came from her mouth how provocative they sounded.

Her partner did not miss his cue. "I am delighted to hear it," he said with lowered voice, and he drew her so close as he whirled her into a turn that she expected at any moment to feel his body against her breasts. "I shall be most conscientious, ma'am, in seeing what I contribute to that enjoyment."

They danced on, their conversation moving into less personal channels. By the time Lord Waite led her in to supper, Felicity felt quite in command of the situation. It was going to be all right. Once the ball had begun, she had felt quite relaxed with all her partners, even with her present one after that disconcerting opening to their conversation. If she could spend time in his company and be herself, then she would be able to do so with anyone. She smiled dazzlingly across the room at Tom, who was handing a plate to a particularly sallow-faced little blonde and seating himself beside her.

Felicity and Lord Waite conversed easily with the other occupants of their table, but long before any other people seemed inclined to leave their places and return to the ballroom, he leaned toward his partner and suggested that they move out of the crush and the heat for a moment. She took his arm and he led her back to the deserted ballroom.

"Ha!" he said. "Still stuffy. We must wander outside, ma'am. There is a terrace beyond the French doors?"

"Yes, indeed," she assured him. "I had the doors left open for the convenience of my guests. By all means let us get some air while we can, my lord. I must be back with my guests when the dancing resumes."

He smiled down at her and touched lightly with his fingers the hand that rested on his arm. "Am I not your guest too, ma'am?" he asked.

He led her along the empty terrace, viewing with a smile the large potted plants that adorned its length at intervals. "I see you have been tactful enough to provide a measure of privacy to your guests as well, ma'am," he said as soon as they moved out of the shaft of light coming through the doors. And he drew her firmly around behind one of the clumps of plants so that her back was against the stone balustrade and Lord Waite in front of her. They were almost totally surrounded by plants and darkness.

"I have waited many years for this opportunity," he said, lifting one long finger to trace the outline of her face. The finger stopped beneath her chin. "You certainly know how to lure a man, Felicity."

She felt that the stone balustrade would pass completely through her spine if she pressed herself against it any more rigidly. "We must return to the ballroom," she said in a voice that sounded surprisingly cool to her own ears. "I am the hostess, my lord, and the chaperone of the twins."

She could see the flash of his teeth as he smiled in the darkness. "I suppose I shall have to endure your teasing," he said. "You lived under restraint for so long, I believe. And I am a patient man, Felicity— within limits, of course. I shall demand only one kiss

tonight. You see, I am capable of great restraint,
too."

His lips were cool, firm on hers. Felicity's hands,
behind her back, gripped the stone rail as if life itself
depended upon her not letting go. His hands lightly
cupped her breasts and moved behind her waist so
that suddenly she was brought hard against him and
his mouth opened over hers. Felicity's hands came
forward and pushed firmly against his shoulders.
She said nothing as she gazed into his pale eyes,
only inches from her own.

"Ah, Felicity," he said, "so beautiful and so full of
fire. But you are right. This is not the time or place.
Go back to your guests. Now more than ever I need
the cool air."

Felicity danced the next few sets in a daze, going
through the motions, smiling, conversing, even taking time to see that her sisters were properly partnered. When Tom came to claim his waltz, it felt like
sailing into a safe haven. She let her hands touch
him and drew calmness and strength from his friendly
words, his kindly smile.

"The twins are well-launched," he said. "You must
be vastly pleased. I fear you are going to be beating
the suitors from the door in the next few weeks."

"Yes, I am delighted," she agreed. "It is so important to me that they find husbands here so that they
can lead more exciting lives than they could have
expected had they stayed at home."

Tom smiled.

"And you, Tom," she said archly, "I thought you
despised *ton* affairs. I expected you to retreat to the
card room at the earliest opportunity, or even to the
library. But you have danced every set. I have been
watching, you see. Perhaps you will find a wife this
Season, too, Tom, and shake off your staid bachelorhood."

"There are far too many to choose from," he protested. "And in this country I would not be allowed
to set up a harem. No, sad as it seems, my dear, I

think it would probably be easier if I retire to the country and my sheep and books when this whirl is over for another year."

"Oh," she said, pulling a face, "I do not believe you, Tom. Why else would you have come to town this year?"

"Perhaps just to witness the success of three of my favorite ladies," he said. "How is this ball going for you, Flick? Do you think you have met that dream husband yet?"

She smiled conspiratorially. "Yes," she said, "I do believe I have, Tom."

He smiled again.

6

Two days later, Felicity was even more convinced that she was right. She sank into the most comfortable sofa in the drawing room and waited for tea to be brought in. It felt good to be alone for once. She was the first to arrive home after an afternoon's drive in the park, Lucy driving with the Earl of Darlington, of all people, and Laura visiting her newly made friend, Lady Pamela Townsend. Felicity stretched her arms above her head and her legs out in front of her. She yawned.

Lord Edmond Waite. Lady Felicity Waite! It did not sound much different from her present name, but she decided that she wanted it. And she wanted him. She was in love for the first time in her life—well, not quite the first time, she conceded. But that first love did not really count. She had been young and naive and had not known what she wanted in life. This was different. Edmond—she savored the name in her mind, though she had never spoken it aloud—was the man with whom she wanted to spend the rest of her life. He was handsome in his own special way, titled, wealthy, intelligent, influential; the list could go on and on. But more than all this, he was attractive. He made her feel alive, full of vitality. Life had seemed infinitely exciting for the last two mornings when she had awoken and thought of him.

The morning after the ball she had not been at all sure that the acquaintance would continue, or, indeed, that she wished it to do so. He had stirred her senses the night before, but he had been outrageously impudent. He barely knew her, yet he had called her by her given name without even asking if he might do so. He had mentioned Wilfred quite disrespectfully. It would have been more appropriate for him to offer his condolences, since he had not seen her since her bereavement. And he had maneuvered her behind those plants on the terrace and kissed her just as if she had been a light-skirts. It had not even been a chaste kiss on the lips. He had pulled her against him so that she had been shockingly aware of his masculinity. And when he had opened his mouth over hers, she had felt herself being drawn into the heat of his desire. No man had ever done that to her before—except once, of course. But that had been different because she had been so emotionally involved in that other embrace that her mind had not been able to stand back and take note of the impropriety of the situation. With Lord Waite she had been very much aware that she should not be doing that. But she had to admit that that very fact had perhaps increased the excitement of the moment.

Felicity had not had long in which to consider her dilemma the day after the ball. A large bouquet of white roses from Lord Waite arrived before luncheon, one of the first of several floral tributes sent to one or other of the three sisters from admirers of the evening before. In the afternoon he had been the first visitor to arrive. He had stayed for almost an hour, conversing most of the time with the twins and with other guests. Felicity had felt a twinge of disappointment until she had found him bowing over her hand, looking at her intently out of those strange pale eyes and asking if he might return at half-past four to drive her in the park.

"I have a new high-perch phaeton to try out,

ma'am," he had said. "If you have a head for heights
and if you trust my driving, I should be honored to
have your company."

Felicity had smiled. "You must know, my lord,
that I am aware you are one of the best whips in
London," she said.

"*One* of the best?" he had queried, and she had
laughed.

It had been absurd for a mere drive in the park to
fill her with such elation. She had felt like a very
young girl out for the first time with a male escort
who was not her father or brother. She had driven
in Hyde Park on numerous previous occasions, often with Wilfred, sometimes with a female companion. And she had always enjoyed viewing the large
variety of carriages and horses and seeing all the
newest fashions being displayed by gentlemen and
ladies alike. She had enjoyed feeling a part of it all,
bowing to acquaintances, sometimes stopping to exchange news or gossip. But she had never before felt
that she was at the heart of all the activity, that all
attention was somehow focused on her and her
companion.

He had somehow made her feel as if he were
aware only of her, although he had driven slowly
around the park, stopping frequently to talk to other
members of the *ton* who were bent on the same
pursuits. And Felicity had felt her cheeks glowing,
her eyes sparkling, her mouth constantly smiling.
She felt like a new woman and was convinced that
the *beau monde* was seeing the real Lady Wren for the
first time.

"Felicity," he had said at one point, "you are truly
beautiful, you know. At one time I thought perhaps
it all depended upon that glorious golden hair. But
even with most of it hidden beneath that absurd
little bonnet, you easily put into the shade every
other lady in the park. You must know that I am the
envy of every other male in sight."

"My lord," she had protested, "you put me to the

blush. How can I answer to such outrageous compliments?"

He smiled and his eyes strayed from hers to her lips. "You are, in addition to your beauty, quite adorable," he had said. "I would kiss you if this were not such an infernally public place. I have a party of people coming with me to Vauxhall Gardens tomorrow evening to share my box. But now I find the prospect quite empty unless you say that you will come too. Will you, Felicity?"

Her heart had turned over. Incredible as it seemed, she had been to the gardens only once, with Wilfred. He had guarded her particularly closely on that occasion because the place was notorious as a pleasure garden where lower classes were likely to be and where young bucks frequently picked up lightskirts. He had even instructed her to refuse all invitations to dance. But she had been enchanted by the sheer romance of the setting—lawns and walks and trees next to the river, all lit by lanterns, the dancing area with its tiers of boxes forming a semicircle around it. She had ached to be free to run and dance and explore. And now to be invited there by the most romantic figure in all of London!

"I am afraid, my lord," she had said, "that Mr. Russell is to take my sisters and me to the opera tomorrow night. There is a new tenor at Covent Garden, you know, who is rapidly becoming all the rage."

"And he will continue to be so for weeks to come," Lord Waite had answered. "Allow Russell to take your sisters there. Two lovely ladies for one man are more than enough, anyway. And who is this Russell, Felicity? Anyone I need be jealous of?"

"Tom?" she had asked, and her smile softened unconsciously. "He is my father's neighbor and the most dear friend I have in the world."

"Friend?"

"Friend."

"Well, Felicity," he said, "may I never be cursed

with the honor of being called your friend. Now, about Vauxhall. Will you come?"

"Yes, I will," she had said, feeling only the smallest twinge of guilt.

Tom had not objected. She had told him that morning when they had ridden together in the almost deserted park.

"Will you mind ever so much if I do not accompany you tonight?" she had asked as their horses cantered side by side. "I have been invited to Vauxhall Gardens, you see, and I very much want to go."

"Someone special, Flick?" he had asked quietly.

"Lord Waite," she had replied. "Do you know him, Tom?"

"The very tall fellow with the aristocratic nose?" he had asked. "Yes, I know him. I watched him win five thousand from some poor devil at cards one night. Years ago. Is he the one you were bubbling over the other night?"

"He is most charming," she had said, her cheeks flushing, only partly as a result of the breeze blowing against them, "and he pays me the most outlandish compliments. Oh, Tom, I do believe I am falling in love."

"In that case," he had said with a smile, "I think I had better excuse you tonight. Those little brats will be enough of a handful, anyway, especially now, when half the male population of London are acquainted with them and will doubtless crowd your box during each interval to play the game of guess-which-is-which."

"Poor Tom," she had said with a laugh. "You really are a dear, you know, to spend so much of your time watching over us. But you really must not ruin your own Season, Tom. I am sure there are a number of girls who danced with you the other night and who would be delighted to further the acquaintance. I should so like to see you well-settled."

"The trouble with you, Flick," he had said, "is that those twins have aroused your matchmaking instincts. You confine your efforts to them, my dear girl. I shall look after my own interests." But he had grinned at her to show that he was not seriously scolding.

The twins, too, had not minded. It seemed to them a delightful adventure to be going to the opera without the chaperonage of their sister, with only Mr. Russell to watch over them.

So Felicity sat now, sipping at her tea and sampling one of Cook's jam tarts and smiling happily. More white roses had appeared that morning and again she had been invited to drive in the park, although she would be seeing him that evening. At this rate, she thought, she could almost expect a declaration this evening, though surely not. It must be far too soon. She had looked forward to an exciting Season, but had certainly not expected things to be quite this easy.

Felicity's peaceful rest was not to last long. The twins arrived home almost at the same moment.

"Well, did you two have a good afternoon?" Felicity asked.

"Lady Pamela is such a good friend," Laura said. "She does not put on airs for all that her grandfather is a duke."

"The earl drove me for more than an hour in the park," Lucy said, "and introduced me to several people I had not met before. They all seemed to know that I have a twin."

"She lives in a lovely house," Laura continued. "You should just see the grounds. They are more like a park. But then, you will seem them. Lady Townsend is to give a garden party soon and we are all to be invited."

"We met Viscount Varley," Lucy said, and giggled. "He raised his hat and said, 'Good day to you, Miss Laura-Lucy.' "

"Lady Townsend says she has heard we will be

sent vouchers for Almack's soon," Laura said. "Oh, I do hope so. I long to go there."

"Do you think we will be allowed to waltz soon?" Lucy asked, coming out of her own dreams far enough to notice what her sister was saying. "When I told the earl that we had been taking lessons, he begged for the honor of being the first to waltz with me. Imagine, Laura!"

Felicity finally shooed them upstairs to rest for half an hour before getting ready for dinner and the opera. She followed them up, a spring in her step. Tom was coming to dinner. His conversation would relax her before Lord Waite came to escort her in his carriage.

Tom was not looking forward with such eagerness to dinner. In fact, he was beginning to wonder why on earth he had come to London and why he was staying. Did he enjoy pain? Over the years he had learned to handle his own feelings. He had admitted to himself years before that he would never be a thoroughly happy man. But having accepted that basic premise, he had proceeded to organize his life so that it would bring him contentment, at least. That contentment had been shattered, of course, with the arrival of Felicity. But he had expected that. He had allowed for it. For two weeks he could endure the sweet pain of seeing her and talking to her and knowing that she no longer cared for him in the way he loved her. He could have endured it many times, whenever she came home to pay visits. It was not likely to be a very frequent occurrence.

But now he had deliberately and foolishly decided to prolong his contact with her. And he had cut himself off from the one thing that could ensure a certain tranquillity of mind: his land. He did not belong here. He found a day of social activity in town far more tiring than a day spent working elbow to elbow with his farm laborers. He felt uncomfortable with the leading lights of society, those who took and enjoyed all that the various entertainments offered. And he pitied those who were on the fringes but obviously unhappy because they could never hope to be at the center of attention. He had felt a desperate tenderness for all those girls at Felicity's ball who were trying to appear either deliberately bored or gay, when it was perfectly obvious that their cards were not full. He had found them pathetically grateful to be asked to dance and to be talked to during the process.

But here he was, not enjoying himself and wounded afresh every time he saw Felicity. She was so totally unaware of his feelings, so eager to twist the knife in his wounds, without being at all aware, of course, that there was either a wound or a knife. As he stood before the mirror in his bedchamber tying his neckcloth into its simple knot and brushing his hair, which he must remember to have cut one of these days, he admitted ruefully to himself that he had almost hoped that Felicity would not find what she was looking for. He did not wish her ill, he did not wish her unhappiness, but he had hoped, without ever admitting it to himself until this moment, that she would turn to him again.

Well, it was not to be. And she had set her sights on Waite. Tom could have hoped for a better choice. He knew no real ill of the man, but he was the kind of aristocrat to whom Tom felt most averse. The man was haughty. Tom doubted that he even acknowledged the existence of any mortal whom he considered less than himself. And he lacked compassion. On that occasion when Tom had witnessed him winning five thousand pounds from an opponent at cards, Waite had not so much as looked at the defeated man. But Tom had, and he had hardly slept that night. He had heard a few weeks later that the same man was in debtor's prison. The fact about Waite that most made Tom uneasy, though, was that he had heard the man was a habitual womanizer. And he had heard, quite by accident, since coming to town, that the man was all but engaged to a Lady Somebody-or-other. Was he merely toying with Felicity's affections? And even if not, even if he married her, would he remain faithful?

The thought of another man being unfaithful to Felicity brought a grim look to Tom's face. He jerked on his evening coat with unnecessary violence. Just let him try! The man might be wonderfully adept with a sword or a pistol—he probably had nothing better to do with his time than practice those skills. But Tom would bet that he was more than an even match for Waite at fisticuffs. He would just love the opportunity to draw the man's cork.

He laughed suddenly in self-derision. He was thinking of the man Felicity was falling in love with, the man who had brought that sparkle to her face that had so pained him this morning. She was no girl. She was a woman of some maturity and experience. He was sure she would make a wise choice. And what did it matter if he disapproved? Who was he? Just a jealous fool.

Tom left his rooms and decided to walk the mile to her house. Above all, he had to appear calm and cheerful when he arrived. She seemed genuinely to value his presence and his friendship, and he could not let her down by giving her any suspicion that he was really just a poor little puppy who had to follow her shadow wherever she went. He would not go home. He would be here for her in whatever capacity she needed him. And when she married, as she very well might do soon—well, then would be time enough to go back home again to lick his wounds. He would have the rest of a lifetime in which to restore his tranquillity.

They entered Vauxhall Gardens from the river, and Felicity was thoroughly enchanted, as she had expected to be. The colors from the lanterns strung through the trees danced in the ripples of the water.

And Lord Waite sat at her elbow, watching her in some amusement.

"How refreshing your company is, Felicity," he said. "You must have experienced almost all the amusements that Europe has to offer, yet you continue to show delight at the sight of a place you must have visited a dozen times."

"Oh, but the company one is in makes all the difference," she said, watching the boat pull in to the landing stage. It was only when Lord Waite was silent and she turned to look inquiringly into his face that she realized she had said those words aloud. She blushed, but she doubted that he would notice that in the artificial light of the lanterns. She turned away in some confusion from the look in his eyes.

Their companions were one other couple, somewhat older than themselves and preoccupied with each other's company. Felicity had been somewhat surprised when introductions were made to find that they were not a married couple. But now she could hardly remember their names and felt no real desire to know them better. She was aware only of the man strolling beside her, her arm linked through his. He looked quite magnificent tonight, she thought, a black evening cloak covering black evening clothes. Almost satanic, in fact. She felt quite sorry for all the other ladies they passed. How could they be enjoying themselves when they were not with him? She almost laughed aloud at her own absurdity.

"A penny for them, Felicity," he said quietly from beside her. "Can you share the joke with me?"

She laughed aloud. "I was merely thinking what a lovely evening it is," she said, "and how I should love to dance."

"Then dance we shall," he said, covering with a warm hand the fingers that were resting on his arm, "after which we shall sit in my box and have some wine. I must let the whole world see that I am escorting the most lovely lady in the gardens tonight."

They danced. Why was it, Felicity wondered, that

music sounded so much more heavenly out of doors
and that one's feet seemed to move so much more
lightly? Why was one so much more aware of one's
partner, of his body heat reaching out to envelop
one, his hand firmly enclosing one's own, his breath
warm on one's cheek? She raised her eyes to his.

"Perhaps we should leave the wine for later," he
murmured. "I am sure that Peter and his lady will
not mourn our absence for a while. Shall we walk?"

It felt strange to be able to step out of the brighter
lights of the dancing area to walk along a shadier
path with this man without first having to look around
to secure permission from someone to do so. Felicity
felt dazzled for a moment by her own sense of freedom and offered no resistance at all even when her
companion led her out of the main promenades and
into the narrower paths where the branches of the
trees met and whispered above their heads and where
the lanterns were fewer and farther between. He
drew her arm close against his so that her shoulder
rested against his arm. She still did not resist. She
delighted in the feeling of excitement growing inside
her. She wondered if he would kiss her again.

She did not have to wonder for long. When they
had walked for several minutes and passed only two
couples, he drew her off the path and around behind the trunk of a large tree. They were instantly in
almost total darkness. And it was quiet except for
the sound of the breeze in the treetops and the very
distant sounds of music and laughter.

He leaned his back against the tree without a
word and drew her to him. Her body was angled
forward slightly so that her feet would not bear her
own weight. She leaned against him, relying on him
entirely for support.

"Felicity," he whispered against her ear, "you have
utterly enslaved me. I cannot do without you any
longer."

She closed her eyes and leaned her forehead against
his chest.

"You feel as I do, do you not?" he said. "Tell me I have not been imagining your response."

"Yes," she whispered, "no." She raised her head and laughed.

He caught her head between his hands and kissed her hungrily. His mouth was open, demanding a response. One hand moved down to hold her firmly behind the hips and bring her hard against him.

Felicity jerked back, her legs shaking suddenly.

"Yes, yes," he said, taking her shoulders in his hands and bringing her against him more gently, "I have no sense of propriety at all when I touch you. It is a good thing you have a cooler head, Felicity, on both this occasion and the last. Come, we shall go to my house."

"Your house?" she echoed.

"Oh, not my main residence," he said, touching her cheek gently. "I keep a house for more private occasions. Don't worry, love, my staff behaves with the utmost discretion. They would lose their positions else."

Felicity swallowed. "You want me to come there with you now?" she asked.

He laughed softly. "The ground beneath our feet would not make a soft rest for your back, love," he said, "especially with my weight on top of you. We need a soft bed in which to make love. I want it to be perfect the first time."

Felicity was grateful for the darkness. She felt deeply shocked and did not know what to say or do. Had she led an even more sheltered life with Wilfred than she had realized? Was it usual for men to take to bed the ladies they intended to marry, even before the wedding ceremony? Surely not. What if something happened to prevent the ceremony? And when would he tell her that he wanted her as a wife?

"You have other guests, my lord," she said. "It would be ill-mannered to abandon them."

He chuckled. "They have probably abandoned us

by now, love," he said. "Peter does not often have the chance of a whole evening alone with his mistress. He has a jealous wife."

Felicity felt her heart begin to beat uncomfortably. "The twins will be home from the opera soon," she said. "They will wait up to tell me about it. I should be home soon."

"Can they not contain their excitement until tomorrow morning?" he asked.

"Everything is so new to them, you see," she explained. "And Tom will perhaps wait to assure me that all went well during the evening."

Lord Waite suddenly laughed aloud, planted a kiss on her cheek, and drew her back onto the path, which seemed brightly lit in comparsion with the almost total darkness from which they had emerged.

"I perceive you are a tease, Felicity," he said, his pale eyes roaming her body from head to toe. "You mean to put me off, do you not?"

She had retreated behind her usual mask. Her lips half-smiled as she regarded him from beneath drooped eyelids. "Really, my lord," she said, "we hardly know each other."

He laughed again. "I have just presented you with the opportunity to rectify that situation," he said. "But I can see that you wish to raise my desire to fever pitch. Play your little game, my love. I shall enjoy the process. I shall enjoy even more the delight of bedding you when you finally decide that you are ready to become my mistress."

He extended an arm to her. Felicity took it, head and heart thumping behind the placid smile she presented to the world for the hour that elapsed before Lord Waite kissed her hand before her own front door, which an impassive footman held open.

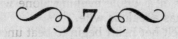

7

The twins had waited up for Felicity, though Tom had not stayed. He had merely seen them over their own threshold and had gone riding off again in the carriage, they told her. But Felicity was not in a good mood to deal with their high spirits. She shooed them off to bed, yawning loudly to convince them that she was exhausted, and promised that she would listen to all they had to say the next morning.

They certainly forced her to keep her promise. She went into the garden after breakfast to examine her rose bushes. Wilfred had had them planted the year after their marriage, when he knew that she loved roses—dozens and dozens of bushes of different varieties and colors of blooms. It was too early in the year to expect any flowers, of course, but she could check to see that they had been properly tended and pruned in the nearly two years since she had been last in residence. The twins trailed her around.

"The Earl of Darlington came to our box to pay his respects to Lucy," Laura announced. "I believe he has a *tendre* for her."

"Oh, stupid," Lucy said modestly.

"It is true," her twin insisted. "Only a few days since our come-out and already he has singled you out for marked attention. He knows her, too, Felicity. Can you imagine? When we saw him coming last night, we decided to play a little trick. I smiled my best smile at him while Lucy looked down over the balcony as if his visit did not concern her at all. He bowed to me, very civil, and I thought, Ha, ha! You have been caught, my man. But then he turned to Lucy, smiled in the most disarming way, took her hand, and kissed it. I was most chagrined."

"No, you were not," Lucy said. "You laughed loudly so that the powdered lady in the next box gave you a look and fanned herself vigorously. And you told the earl what we had been about. Then *I* was chagrined. I wished the box would open beneath my feet and send me plummeting into the pit."

"Well, then, love," Felicity said, viewing her favorite bush, the one that produced peach-colored roses, with her head on one side, "perhaps you should not have been a party to such a trick. Do you think this bush is a little too bushy?"

"But we always play it on new acquaintances," Lucy protested. "It is our way of discovering whether someone is worth developing a friendship with or not."

"And the Earl of Darlington passed the test," Felicity said. "Tell me, Lucy, do you like him? I confess I have never had much to do with the man myself."

Lucy thought for a moment and crinkled her nose. "Yes," she said, "I like him well enough. He is good-looking, even though I do not usually admire blond men. And he is flatteringly attentive. But, you see, I am dazzled mostly by his title. I can hardly believe that an earl, a real honest-to-goodness earl, had singled me out and taken me driving and visited my box at the opera. I shall have to be very careful not to fancy myself in love with the man when perhaps it is the title I might fall for."

Felicity looked at her sister, startled. She had grown to love her sisters very dearly in the past weeks, but while she had not considered them exactly silly, she had thought of them as quite scatterbrained and lacking in maturity. Lucy's extremely common-sense answer to her question amazed and impressed her. And she had thought Lucy the more flighty of the two.

"Poor Viscount Varley did not pass the test," Laura was saying, and both girls were giggling as if they had never entertained a sensible thought in their lives.

"The poor man came mincing into the box," Lucy said, imitating the gait of an accomplished dandy so well that Felicity was forced to join in the laughter. Lucy played up to her audience my miming the viscount's manner of smoothing the lace of his cuffs over his hands and toying with the handle of his quizzing glass. "He made a very elegant leg," Lucy continued, mimicking the action again, "smiled the smile he must have practiced for weeks before his looking glass, and said to Laura, 'Miss Laura? Miss Lucy?' And then he turned to me and said the same thing. We were horrid to him, Felicity, indeed we were. Mr. Russell scolded us roundly for it afterward. He will probably tell you about it."

"We said nothing," Laura said, taking up the story, "absolutely nothing. And we did not crack a smile between us. We have done it before, you know, and it always succeeds in disconcerting a person so. Has Mama told you that we once got rid of a governess after only five days by doing it to her constantly? Anyway, the viscount almost lost his poise. It was a good thing for him that Mr. Russell was there. He stepped forward and told which of us was which in that very quiet way of his and told the viscount that it was just our little joke."

"We were most annoyed with him," Lucy said, "though really, I suppose, he did what was right. Mr. Russell always does what is right. Always! He would be quite dull if he were not such a dear."

"So Viscount Varley has been struck off the list of possible friends and suitors, has he?" Felicity asked, sitting down on a bench.

"Oh, I may give him a second chance," Laura said

airily, "he is so very handsome, you see. Have you ever seen such gorgeous dark, curly hair before, Felicity? And those dark-brown eyes! And that smile. Maybe he has practiced it, Lucy, but you must admit that the result is quite devastating. It turns me quite weak at the knees."

"Pooh," Lucy said, "he's just a popinjay."

"Lady Pamela told me that he has quite a reputation as a swordsman," Laura said, annoyed. "He even fought a duel once and severely wounded his opponent, though it was all hushed up. And did you notice the muscles of his calves, Lucy?"

"I am not in the habit of going around noticing gentlemen's legs," Lucy said, and dissolved into giggles.

Her twin turned from her in disgust. "How was your evening, Felicity?" she asked.

Felicity had shrugged off the question with the sort of answer that her sisters expected. But truth to tell, memories of the evening before ruined her day. She might have shrugged it all off if a bouquet of white roses had not arrived from Lord Waite for the third morning in a row. She had somehow assumed that her refusal of the night before to go to his house and submit to being made love to would have made him forget her instantly. But obviously not. She grabbed the vase of flowers, which someone on her staff had already arranged and set in the morning room, marched with it down to the kitchen, and demanded that the flowers be thrown away immediately. How had he managed to get roses anyway, when her own rose bushes told her quite distinctly that it was too early yet for anything but leaves and thorns?

If he sent roses, he would quite possibly have the audacity to visit during the afternoon and even to ask her to drive out with him again. So Felicity was forced to spend the afternoon in her own apartments with a book when she really felt no inclination at all to read. The butler was instructed to tell all callers that she was in bed with a headache. It was most provoking. She had to ask the housekeeper to take her mending with her into the drawing room and sit in the window seat so that the twins would be properly chaperoned should visitors arrive.

The twins came tiptoeing into her sitting room later in the afternoon. They were quite convinced by the headache story. There seemed to be no other reason why their sister would sit upstairs rather than in the drawing room, where she might have been entertained. Felicity kept up the pretense when she found out that Lord Waite had come, had asked for her, and had stayed only fifteen minutes. Drat the man! Now she would have to miss the evening's engagement, too. Having denied her presence in her own drawing room on the grounds that she was ill, she could hardly attend the dinner and social gathering at the home of Lady Pelman that she had accepted. She did not believe that Lord Waite was invited to that gathering, but she could not risk other people's finding out and considering her lacking in good breeding. For the second night in a row she would have to entrust the twins to Tom's care.

Tom had agreed to escort the girls, though he had felt definite disappointment yet again that Felicity was not to be with them. He had always had something of a soft spot for the twins, perhaps because they were her sisters. And although they looked nothing like her, their high spirits and talkativeness reminded him of the way she had been as a girl. He had not had much to do with them, of course. At home they were too young for his friendship. But he had always enjoyed their prattle whenever he visited the Maynards, and he always derived amusement from the way they would nudge each other and suppress giggles, especially if there was a strange young man present.

And he enjoyed their company now in London. It

relaxed the tedium of his days to watch them become transformed into fashionable and very pretty young ladies, and to note the male attention that they drew wherever they went. He approved of the way they did not simper or preen themselves before all the attention. They had a basic good sense that set them to analyzing every situation they met and that developed in them a disconcerting habit of ridiculing anyone they suspected of insincerity.

The night before, when they had so mercilessly set down that conceited Varley, Tom had had to suppress a powerful urge to shout with laughter. His kindlier nature had prevailed. He had smoothed over the situation and released Varley from his embarrassing predicament. He hated to see other people feel or look ridiculous. Tom possessed too strongly the ability to identify with others, to understand how they were feeling. But he had to give those girls credit. Almost any other debutante would have swooned quite away at one admiring glance or one of those practiced smiles from the viscount.

On the way to the Pelmans' house, Tom allowed the girls to do all the talking, an indulgent smile on his face. He knew that Felicity was too sick with the headache to come; they had told him that when he had arrived to escort them. But he learned on the journey that it was a strange headache. When the girls had gone to her room before dinner, she had actually been reading a book, and when they had gone up to kiss her good night before leaving with him, she had been working on her embroidery. Was she really unwell, he wondered, or was there some other reason for her staying at home? At first, Tom thought that perhaps she was avoiding him. It was, after all, the second evening on which she had canceled an engagement with him. But he did not think so. The morning of the day before, when they had ridden together, they had parted on the usual friendly terms. And she had been fairly talkative during dinner the evening before. He was quite sure that he had not on any occasion let slip his real feelings for her.

The problem nagged at Tom all through dinner and in the drawing room afterward while he stood beside the pianoforte bench and turned the pages of music for the young lady whose dinner companion he had been and who seemed to have appropriated him as her own private property. Finally he had an idea. Laura was sitting almost head to head with her new friend, Lady Pamela Townsend. Lucy was settling herself at a card table with three other people. Her partner, Tom noticed with interest, was the Earl of Darlington. He singled out Lady Townsend, excused himself from the pianoforte player, and crossed the room to her side. A few whispered words and she was nodding quite firmly. Of course there was room in her carriage for the Misses Maynard and of course she would be quite delighted to keep a motherly eye on them for the rest of the evening and convey them safely home. If Mr. Russell had remembered a pressing appointment, then certainly he must keep it.

Fifteen minutes later, Tom was being admitted to the house on Pall Mall. He was not at all sure that he was doing the right thing. If Felicity really were sick, then she would certainly not thank him for disturbing her at this rather late hour of the evening. Perhaps she would not welcome his presence, anyway. He gave instructions to the butler that Lady Wren wa not to be disturbed if she was already asleep. But if she was still up, he would be obliged for a few minutes of her time.

Two minutes later, as Tom was pacing the hallway, Felicity herself came tripping down the stairs, her hands extended to him in greeting. "Tom," she said warmly, "how lovely of you to come. How did you know that I need your company so much this evening? Do come up to the drawing room. Where are the twins? John, would you send some claret up for Mr. Russell, please?"

"Well, Flick," Tom said a few minutes later when they were settled alone in the drawing room, "are you going to tell me what your headache is all about?"

She smiled wryly. "I might have known that you would know it is not a real headache," she said. "Oh, Tom, I am so miserable."

"Waite?" he asked gently. "Did the evening not go well?"

"Oh, it went beautifully," she said, jumping to her feet and crossing to the fireplace. She stood with one arm resting on the mantel, her fingers drumming on its marble surface. "We danced, Tom, and we walked. And you could not imagine a more romantic setting. Lanterns and moonlight and trees and shady walks. Music. Have you ever been to Vauxhall? And he kissed me, Tom, and I was convinced he was about to propose marriage to me, absurd as it seems when we have been acquainted really for only a few days. Well, he did propose." The drumming of her fingers became louder and faster.

"Did he?" Tom prompted. "And you did not accept?"

"Tom," Felicity said. The drumming had become frantic. "I think I am going to cry. And I almost never cry. If I stop talking, my face will crumple up and I shall start bawling. And I shall feel very foolish. I think you had better—"

Tom was on his feet and beside her before she could either continue or carry out her threat. He took her firmly by the shoulders and pulled her against him. He held her head against his neckcloth.

"Stop talking, Flick," he said, "and let yourself cry if you must. You need not be ashamed to do so in my presence, you know. I am your friend, remember? There, there, love. Cry your heart out. I can hold you for as long as you need." He cradled her in his arms and rocked her gently, crooning comforting words into her ear while she sobbed against his chest and held his lapels in tight fists.

She sniffed finally and released her hold of his coat. "Oh, dear," she mumbled into his neckcloth, "I have made you all wet, Tom." Her hands were smoothing over his crumpled lapels.

"No harm done," he said. "Here, take my handkerchief and dry your eyes and blow your nose. No, you don't have to hide your face from me, Flick. Here, let me do it. It's probably red and blotchy, is it? People's faces usually are after they have had a good cry. I won't mind. There, you don't look that bad. Your nose is the worst. Quite a beacon." He tapped it with one finger.

She laughed shakily. "Oh, Tom," she said, "you are a dear. You make everything seem so ordinary. Already I feel as if I have been acting like a perfect goose all day."

"I don't expect you have," he said. "Something pretty serious happened to upset you last night. Come, let's sit over here and you shall put your head on my shoulder and tell me all about it."

"Oh, may I?" she said gratefully. "I always feel so safe when I am close to you, Tom, as if nothing in the world had the power to hurt me or even bother me. You will take care of it all. Is not that absurd?"

"Very," he agreed, adjusting his arm around her shoulders so that her head lay comfortably on his shoulder. "But I'll always help you whenever I can, Flick, you know that."

There was a short silence during which her hand crept to his lapel again. "He did not propose marriage," she said. "He wants me to be his mistress, Tom."

The muscles of the arm that lay beneath her neck tightened somewhat. "Are you sure?" he asked.

"Oh, yes," she replied. "He actually used the word. He wanted me to go with him then to his house. Not his home, you understand, but a house he keeps for his mistresses."

"Did you tell him quite firmly no?" Tom asked.

"No, I did not. I made excuses for last night. Said

I had to be home soon because you and the twins would be waiting for me. But I just sort of hedged on the other. I thought he might interpret my behavior as being a definite rejection, but he sent me flowers again today and came visiting this afternoon. That is why I pretended the headache, you see. I could not see him."

"I should call the fellow out for this," Tom said fiercely. "How dare anyone make such improper advances to you!"

"Oh, no, indeed you must not, Tom," Felicity said anxiously, raising her head and looking into his face. "Perhaps he had reason, you see. I have been trying all last night and today to recall if I have said or done anything to make him think that that is the sort of relationship I seek. Perhaps I am too old to make a man's mind turn toward marriage. Or maybe because I am wealthy and have several lovely homes and carriages and such, Lord Waite has assumed that I am happy enough. All I need to complete my contentment is a lover."

"I might have known this would happen," Tom said. "I didn't say anything to you, Flick, because you were so happy and I thought the man would be a fool if he was not sincere, but he has quite a reputation with the ladies. And it seems quite certain that he is about to be betrothed to a Lady Somebody-or-other. It's one of those alliances that have been arranged from the cradle, apparently. He has just been waiting for the girl to grow up."

"Is that so?" Felicity commented, her head very still against his shoulder.

"Well, Flick," Tom said cheerfully, "not much harm has been done, you know. As you just said, it is only a few days since Waite started to pay court to you. It's very early in the Season yet, and there are many other eligible bachelors who look as if all they need is a little encouragement. Before you know it, you will have found someone else and be just as happy as you were when I met you yesterday morning."

"Is that so?" Felicity said again, just as if Tom had said nothing in the meanwhile. She pushed herself away from his shoulder and sat upright next to him. "So he thought to set up a very comfortable nest, did he? A young wife, aristocratic like him, no doubt, someone eminently suitable to grace his home and produce his heirs. And me on the side to provide his pleasure. Me, the daughter of a mere country gentleman of modest means and widow of a man who made his fortune and his title in business. Not worthy of his illustrious name, of course, but perfectly acceptable for his bed. Well, we shall see, Lord High-and-mighty Waite. We shall see!"

Tom got to his feet. "Don't get yourself upset, Flick," he said. "He is not worth it. There will be plenty of men to appreciate you, even worship you, for what you are. You aren't harboring a real *tendre* for the man, are you?"

"I don't know," she replied. "I have felt so many different ways about him in the last few days, and all of the feelings intense. I really do not know whether I love him or hate him or feel quite indifferent to him. But I do know one thing, Tom: you are looking at the future Lady Waite. It is the poor girl, Lady Something-or-other, who had better look around her for someone else. I mean to have him."

"I say," Tom said, passing a hand along the back of his neck above his collar. "Do you think this is wise, Flick?"

She sat back and folded her arms. She smiled at him, her eyes dancing with the idea that was forming in her mind. "I think I am about to enjoy myself immensely," she said. "He called me a tease. He has seen nothing yet. I shall tease him and torment him, encourage him and repulse him until he can think only of making me his wife."

"Flick," Tom said uneasily, "I don't think you know quite what you are about. You are not dealing with some green youth, you know. You will be playing with fire if you mean to tease Waite."

"Then you shall help me," she said. "The trouble is, you see, Tom, that I do not know much about enticing a man. But you must have all kinds of experience. You have not lived the life of a monk all these years, have you? You can teach me how I can best wrap a man around my little finger. Will you, Tom?"

"Good Lord!" he said. He scratched his head. "Good Lord, Flick, what do you take me for? You know far more than I do. You are the one who has been married, you know."

"Oh, yes," she said, making a dismissive gesture with her hand, "but that does not count. Wilfred never . . ." She flushed. "Well, he, we . . . Oh, look, Tom, you must help me. I do not even know how I ought to kiss. Should I, for example, allow the man to open his mouth when he kisses me? And should I open mine? Will I be thought much too fast if I do? Would it be more enticing to keep my lips firmly closed?"

"Good Lord, Flick," Tom said, utterly embarrassed. "You ought not to let that toad anywhere near you. If he kissed your fingers it would be gross presumption."

"Oh!" she said, her face lighting up suddenly. "I have a splendid idea, Tom. I shall make him jealous. I shall pretend that you and I have a marked *tendre* for each other. Let him think that you are my lover even, perhaps. Yes, that would be just the thing. I shall drive him wild. You will do it for me, Tom, will you not? You will playact for my sake? Oh, please, dear, dear Tom?"

"Good Lord!" he said.

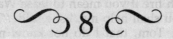

8

Vouchers for Almack's arrived on the same day as invitations to Lady Townsend's garden party. The twins were ecstatic, and Felicity too was pleased. She would not have even thought of bringing her sisters with her to London had they not mentioned it themselves, yet it was so obviously right for them to be here enjoying themselves. And they were certainly doing that. Both had made friends among the other debutantes. Both were much admired by the gentlemen. Never a day passed without some male arriving to visit one or other of them, or all three. The twins never lacked escorts at balls or to take them driving in the park on those occasions when it was not raining.

The game of guessing which twin was which still delighted them and their friends alike. Their closest friends were the ones who could no longer be deceived. The Earl of Darlington had never been fooled, right from the start, and he seemed to be becoming Lucy's accepted suitor. Other men danced with her, conversed with her, and laughed with her, but they stood back whenever the earl approached, as if he had a prior claim on her attention. If he was in the drawing room at Pall Mall during the afternoon, no other man would ask her to go driving.

Felicity wondered about the situation. Were they becoming attached? And was it a good thing if they

were? She would have liked Lucy to have a few
weeks at least in which to be free to get to know
other men. The earl was a quiet, gentlemanly figure,
about her own age, Felicity guessed. He had inher-
ited his father's title and fortune less than two years
before, but she had heard no rumor that his newfound
position and wealth had gone to his head and made
him either conceited or extravagant. Yet her own
recent experience with Lord Waite made her uneasy.
Would the earl raise hopes in Lucy when he had no
intention of ever marrying her? She had nothing to
recommend her to a man of such superior rank except good looks, high spirits, and character.

Laura was far more inclined to enjoy the company
of many but to single out no one for particular favors. The viscount seemed finally to have found a
good method of identifying her. He merely waited
for Darlington to pay his attentions to Lucy and then
noticed the contrast in clothing between the two
girls. For the rest of that particular afternoon or
evening he was safe. The girls usually wore clothes
that were slightly different in shade or design unless
they were in one of their particularly teasing moods.
Varley seemed determined to pay court to Laura,
though she teased him and frequently treated him
quite carelessly.

"He is too handsome for his own good," she explained to Felicity when the latter berated her for
being almost rude one afternoon. "I mean to take
him down a peg or two."

"Is that wise?" Felicity asked. "He may become
altogether disgusted with you and abandon you
entirely."

"Pooh," Laura said, "do you think I should care?"

Felicity too was not ignored. The bouquets of white
roses continued to arrive each morning. Lord Waite
continued to present himself at the house almost
every afternoon. But no longer blinded by that first
burst of flattered admiration for him, she realized
that several other men were interested in her. Tom

had been right. With a little encouragement she could have had several quite ardent suitors. There was Sir Leonard Tully, for example, who had been quite a close acquaintance of her husband's. He had made his fortune and raised himself to gentility in very much the same way as Wilfred. He was a widower in his forties, rather older than she wanted her second husband to be, but it would be a good match. He was elegant, his dark hair graying in just the right places, at his temples. He was a charming man. Felicity allowed him to escort her to the opera one night and to St. James's Park one afternoon.

There was also Mr. Peregrine Hill, a man unquestionably of noble class, though he was untitled. He was in his thirties, she guessed, always impeccably elegant in dress and correct in manner. He was intelligent, cultured, bookish. Whenever he claimed a dance with her, she knew that in fact they would not dance but sit together in a quiet corner and talk intensely about books and art and music. Felicity could contribute quite well to the conversations. Her travels had familiarized her with all that was best in European culture. Her long, frequently lonely days in Wilfred's northern home had made her a reader. She liked Mr. Hill. But she wanted a glittering and exciting life. She had never seen the man smile.

There were others, too, several of them older men who had known Wilfred, several of them all too obviously fortune-hunters.

But there was always Lord Waite, and he prevented her from ever taking any of her prospective suitors seriously. He set the others in the shade. His self-assurance was enormous. He never once appeared put out by the fact that Felicity would accept none of his invitations because she was so busy. He would always bow elegantly over her hand and occasionally kiss it. And he would always look directly at her with pale eyes that laughed at her. He knew she was playing a game with him, knew that she was playing hard to get. But he did not yet know *how* hard to get, she would reflect grimly.

She no longer asked herself if she loved the man. She had not originally set out to allow love to influence her choice, anyway. And she no longer asked herself sanely and rationally if she wished to spend the rest of her life with a man who so clearly used women for his own convenience. She had to have him. Her pride dictated that she bring him to his knees. He would beg and plead with her to marry him before she was finished with him. Lady Dorothea Page—Felicity had quickly found out the identity of "Lady Somebody-or-other"—would have to go husband-hunting on her own account. On the one occasion when Felicity had seen them together, driving in the park when she had been with Tom, they had not looked very loverlike. He had been openly gazing at all the passersby and had looked at her intently, removed his hat, and bowed. She had been looking bored and haughty beneath her blue parasol, not apparently looking at anyone or anything directly.

Felicity was a little uneasy about Tom's role in her plans. It had seemed a perfectly splendid idea when it first popped into her head to use Tom to make Lord Waite jealous. But Tom was her friend and a very dear person. He had not seemed very happy with the idea at first. In fact, he had not actually agreed to become her pretend lover. And, of course, his reason was obvious when she thought about it. Tom's freedom would be severely restricted. If he was to escort her more than ever and appear to have a marked preference for her, then he would no longer be at liberty to look around him to choose a wife. And despite his denials, Felicity was convinced that that must be his reason for being in London. And when it was all over, when she finally became betrothed to Lord Waite, she would leave Tom looking very foolish, just like a jilted lover. No, it was really asking too much of his friendship.

She talked to him about it on the same afternoon as she saw Lord Waite and Lady Page together.

Tom was more than a little uneasy about the scheme into which he was being drawn. First and foremost was his concern for Felicity. She was a strange mixture of experience and naiveté. When he had first met her again after eight years, he had thought her entirely a woman of the world. He would have felt no misgivings about her taking on the most jaded of the country's aristocrats. But now he was not so sure. There was almost a shyness in her that he had felt on more than one occasion, on that first evening, for example, when he had escorted her and the twins to the theater. He would have sworn that all evening she did not once look directly at any other member of the audience. And it was not haughtiness that had held her thus aloof. And then there was that strange manner that she adopted so often when they were in company and she knew she was on display. She seemed to retreat far into herself and gave the impression that she was a cool, sophisticated woman of the world. It was just not Felicity. He knew her as a warm, impulsive, vital person.

Tom wondered about the past eight years. She had certainly been about a great deal and had been part of society. But had she really been a part of it all? Had that husband of hers kept such firm control of the reins that she had not had a chance to become part of her world as an individual? She had said herself that he must help her as he probably had much more experience than she had.

And yet she was planning to play a dangerous game with no less a personage than Lord Waite. Tom had no doubt that it would be highly dangerous. The man was not only experienced with women, he was a person who was very accustomed to having his own way. He would not take kindly to having his affections toyed with. She could not succeed. Tom knew what these long-standing alliances were like. Waite would no more think of not honoring it than he would of backing out of a formal betrothal. Felicity must seem to him the perfect candidate for mistress. She was a widow of independent means. As such, he would not have to keep her under his protection. She was beautiful and desirable. And then there was that unfortunate way she behaved in company. It definitely would give the impression to anyone who did not know her that she had experienced a great deal of life, that she was available to the advances of any man who took her fancy.

Yes, Tom decided, he would have to agree to her suggestion. If he did not, she would carry on with her plan anyway. This way at least he would be able to remain close to her, protect her as much as he could. It would be a difficult role to play, of course, because he must give her the freedom to be alone with Waite long enough to give their relationship a chance to develop along more personal lines. But he must never leave her completely unprotected.

As Tom made his decision, the same night as Felicity proposed the scheme to him, he wished ruefully that it really was no more difficult than his reasoning thus far had made it seem. If only he felt nothing for her, he could play his part with some relish. But how was he to pretend to be her suitor, her lover even, when he really did love her almost to distraction? It would be a doubly ironic situation, and a most painful one for him. How could he possibly be that close to her without letting her see his real feelings? And he must never do that. She loved him dearly as a friend and would be most distressed if she knew that she had hurt him. Their friendship would certainly be destroyed.

It would be so much safer just to pack his bags and go home again, try to resume his life, which had been contented enough until she had come back into it. But he could not, of course. Felicity needed him, and as long as she needed him, he would be there for her. He himself brought up the subject again when they were driving together in the park two days after she had described her mad scheme to him.

"Flick," he said, "are you still bound and determined to marry Waite?"

"Why, yes, of course," she replied. "And I shall, you know."

"I shall do as you ask, then," he said. "You are sitting with your ardent suitor, my love."

"Oh, no, Tom," she protested. "I have been thinking about that. I can do this alone. I do not want to drag you into my affairs. It is only fair that you should be allowed to enjoy the Season on your own account. You will not be able to look for a wife if you are having to moon all over me."

He chuckled. "You are developing into a determined matchmaker," he said. "How many times must I tell you that I am not in search of a wife before you will believe me? I am really not, you know. The more I see of society, the more I know I shall go home when summer comes, quite satisfied with my quiet bachelor existence again. In the meantime, my love, I shall set my sights on you." He leaned closer to her, looked smolderingly into her eyes, and spoke intimately close to her ear. "I find after knowing you again for a few weeks, ma'am, that I have quite lost my heart to you. I beg you to assure me that I am not without hope."

Felicity shot him a startled look and then her eyes twinkled. She tapped him lightly on the hand that held the ribbons. "I am honored by your attentions, sir," she said. "I trust that you will continue to call on me?"

"You will be at Almack's tomorrow night?" Tom said, looking deliberately at her mouth. "Will you reserve two dances for me? Both waltzes?"

"Oh, sir," she said, looking down at her hands, "I should be greatly honored. And, Tom, you had better head your horses away from this squeeze because I can feel a fit of the giggles coming on."

"Not feeling quite the thing, Lady Wren?" he asked, all solicitous concern. "You must allow me to escort you home, ma'am, with all speed."

Lord Waite had not missed the exchange. So that impudent puppy thought he had a chance with her, did he? His lip curled with disdain. Apparently Russell owned the estate adjoining her father's. They had probably grown up together, been childhood sweethearts, perhaps. But she is not for the likes of him now, Lord Waite thought. She has progressed far beyond you, my buck. He did not miss her reaction, either. But he smiled in some amusement as he bent his head to hear some remark his intended made in her bored drawl. Lady Wren knew, of course, that he was there. She had smiled when he bowed to her. She was trying to make him jealous, was she? He did not for a moment believe that she felt any deep emotion for that rather dull country squire.

Lord Waite did not quite understand why Lady Wren had decided to play hard to get. She was probably a born tease. All those years with Wren, when she had seemed a model of propriety, she was probably perfecting the art of conducting very secret amours. And now she was continuing the tactics although there was really no need. No one would particularly censure her now even if news of their affair did become public. And as far as he was concerned, it was now almost expected of him that he take some beautiful lady of the *ton* as his mistress.

However, he was not sorry. It had been a little frustrating, of course, at Vauxhall when he had been so sure of possessing her before the night was out, to find that after all he was doomed to a lonely night of playing cards at Watier's. But he had since warmed to her game. He had no doubt that he would win in the end. Her every glance showed that awareness of him that long practice had taught him was a sure sign of availability. He would possess her before the Season was out, and the final consummation would be all the sweeter for the delay. He felt almost sorry for Russell. Really, it would be a kindness to whisper a hint in his ear.

The twins were somewhat disappointed with Almack's. The ballroom was quite plain in comparison with some of the ballrooms they had already seen. But then, as Felicity explained to them, a private person would give probably only one ball in a year and would therefore take great care to make sure that it was a memorable occasion. Almack's, on the other hand, was open for dancing every week. One could not expect the hostesses to decorate it elaborately each time. Indeed, it was the reputation of the place rather than the place itself that was important. Receiving or not receiving a voucher to Almack's could make or break a social reputation.

And as Laura said with some distaste as they were riding home in the carriage afterward, one could well see why the club was called the marriage mart. There were at least twice as many ladies as men in the ballroom most of the time. The other men were in the card room. And those who were present made their choice of partner with something bordering on insolence, in many cases.

"When a gentleman views one from head to toe across the room through his quizzing glass," Laura said indignantly, "and then proceeds to do the same thing with the girl standing next to one, one feels one might as well be standing on a hustings up for auction."

"Perhaps you should not complain," Felicity said. "You did not have to sit out even one dance, I noticed."

"But plenty of the other poor girls did," her sister said. "I must confess I did not like it at all, Felicity. I do not care if I ever go again."

"I did not mind the dance," Lucy said. "After all, we know that almost every social function of the Season is a marriage market to a certain extent. It seems distasteful to admit it, but we girls are all searching for husbands and many of the men are looking for wives."

"Well, I am not," Laura said crossly. "It sounds quite horrid when you put it like that, Lucy."

"Anyway," her twin said, "what I really objected to was the supper. I was dancing with Darlington, dreaming of lobster patties and oysters. And what did we have? Bread and butter. Bread and butter! Did the caterer forget to order?"

Felicity laughed. "That is the regular fare at Almack's," she said. "It is almost as if the hostesses were trying to ask us how much store we set by appearances. A rather drab setting. Extremely dull food. Stringent rules. Did you know, for example, that even the greatest gentleman will be turned away if he arrives later than eleven o'clock? Or if he is not wearing knee breeches? And yet we all flock there to prove that we are part of the very highest stratum of society."

Felicity waited until she was in her own room, her maid dismissed for the night, a cup of chocolate cooling on the table beside her, before she allowed herself to assess the success of the evening. It had been very satisfactory, she thought with a smile as she hugged her knees and laid her chin on top of them. She had made a good start to her campaign.

She had not been sure that Lord Waite would be there, and felt rather disappointed when he was not as she thought that Tom was looking quite dazzling in dull-gold evening clothes, with a chocolate-brown embroidered waistcoat. And she thought her own white silk gown with gold-embroidered scalloped hem was quite becoming. In fact, it almost seemed that she and Tom must have collaborated on their clothes so that they would complement each other. She had felt quite elated, then, when Lord Waite had come strolling from the card room, quizzing glass in hand, just as Tom was leading her onto the floor for the first of the promised waltzes.

Tom was alerted when she smiled dreamily up at him. He placed a hand firmly behind her waist and pulled her close to him, not too close for propriety, but close enough to suggest a partiality for his partner. He smiled at her with his eyes and held her look while they danced.

Really, Felicity thought now, he was very clever. Tom had hidden depths. She would wager he could charm or seduce any woman he wanted if he just chose to do so. And he was a marvelous dancer. She had not noticed before. He had held her firmly and led unhesitatingly. She had leaned back against his arm, looked into his eyes, and floated. She swore she had not once felt the floor beneath her slippers. She had been almost disappointed when the music came to an end.

But she was quite satisfied that they must have looked most romantic, twirling around the room, with eyes for no one but each other. Strange! With most people one felt uncomfortable making prolonged eye contact, even if conversation was flowing. That was why one usually talked to people next to one rather than across from one at table. Yet she had danced a whole waltz with Tom and would swear they had gazed into each other's eyes the whole while without so much as a moment's embarrassment, only a heady sort of exhilaration.

She had danced with Lord Waite, the supper dance, in fact. He had been all amiability. She had had the uncomfortable feeling that he was laughing at her once or twice, but he had never done so openly.

As usual, he had a disconcerting way of gaining her undivided attention. "Felicity, my dear," he said, "this is the first time I have had the chance to touch more than your fingertips since a certain memorable occasion at Vauxhall. I feel like a man who has staggered through a desert for days and finally found an oasis."

She laughed. "What an extravagant simile, my lord," she said. "You are touching only my waist and my hand, you know." And as usual, she seemed to have an unfortunate habit of saying unintentionally provocative things to him.

"If you are complaining, Felicity," he said, his pale eyes mocking her, "you have no one but yourself to blame. Anytime you say the word, my dear, I shall gladly touch you in more satisfactory places."

She gave him her famous half-smile.

"Ah, what a shame," he said. "I thought for a moment that we were making progress at last. But you are on the retreat. That is not the way you looked at a certain Mr. Russell an hour ago, Felicity. I am *green* with envy, you know."

She looked at him suspiciously from behind her mask. Was he mocking her? "Tom?" she said carelessly. "We have known each other forever. He is a dear friend, you know."

"Yes," he replied, "I do know, and perhaps you had better tell him, in the interests of his health, that he had better not overstep the bounds of friendship." He was definitely laughing now, though there was no particular smile on his face.

"What a pile of nonsense you talk, my lord," she said in her aloof manner.

"But I do mean it, Felicity," he said as the music drew to a close and he tucked her arm through his to lead her in to supper. "You are mine, my dear. You know it and I know it. I trust that Russell will soon share our knowledge." He was smiling.

Yes, Felicity thought, giving her knees a final hug and reaching for her chocolate, a most satisfactory start to the campaign.

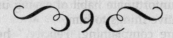

Laura was, as always, the letter writer and the letter reader. She wrote home at least once a week to inform Mama of all their activities and all their purchases. She reported that Mama had written complaining about how quiet the house was without any of her children at home and without even Mr. Russell to pay his frequent calls. Laura wrote to her brother Cedric and reported on receiving a reply that her sister-in-law was in a delicate way.

"Now we shall *have* to find husbands before the summer is over," Lucy commented when she heard the news. "How dreadful it would be to be maiden aunts, Laura. I should feel positively middle-aged."

And it was Laura who wrote to Adrian to inform him that they were in town for the Season. Back came a letter so full of loneliness and homesickness that both twins begged Felicity to invite him for a weekend.

"The poor child will pine quite away if we do not rescue him for just a short while," Laura begged.

"Surely they allow the poor boy to leave that prison house at least for a weekend during term time," Lucy added. "Do write to the headmaster, Felicity."

"What?" their sister said, laughing. "Eton a prison house? If you just knew what a place of privilege it is! I rather suspect that Master Adrian, as youngest in the family, has been a mite spoiled." However, she was anxious herself to see this brother who had been only a child of ten when she had last seen him. The letter was written and it was arranged that the boy could leave the school on Friday and return on Sunday provided a relative accompanied him on both occasions. As the twins pointed out, his visit would help break the tedium of too many social events piled one on another. By the time he returned to school, the Townsend garden party would be almost upon them.

Tom agreed to devote much of his weekend, too, to entertaining the youngest Maynard. "What?" he said when the twins first told him the news. "That brat is coming to your home, Flick? Heaven help you. The place will never be the same again."

"Is he that bad?" she asked dubiously.

"Worse. He is that type of odious child who likes to play practical jokes, and there is not an original one in his whole repertoire. Just last summer, for example, when he was in my stables supposedly helping the groom, he waited until he saw me approach and yelled 'Fire!' in a good imitation of panic. When I went charging through the stable door, not only did I trip over a piece of string that had been stretched across the doorway, but I had a pail of oats that had been balanced on top of the door dumped on my head. Fortunately, the pail itself missed me or I do believe I might have taken my whip to the brat's hide."

"Oh, dear," said Felicity.

He arrived duly in the late afternoon of Friday, having been fetched by Felicity herself and Tom. He seemed somewhat awed when he saw what a grand lady his sister was. Even Tom looked so much more the gentleman in his town finery that Adrian was almost tongue-tied. During the journey to Pall Mall, he spoke only when spoken to and asked after his sisters with the utmost politeness. Felicity began almost to think that school had broken the poor lad's spirit until she met Tom's eyes across the carriage. He pulled a comical face at her and winked.

Less than an hour later, Felicity was almost wishing that they were back in that carriage with a subdued, polite schoolboy. When they entered the house on Pall Mall and the twins came running downstairs to throw themselves on their brother, he immediately came out of his trance. Even before they had all climbed the staircase to the drawing room, they had heard about how wicked a place Eton was—work and prep and more work, older boys that bullied and domineered, masters who were unfeeling tyrants, food that closely resembled sawdust and pig swill, buildings that must rival Newgate for gloominess.

"I say, Felicity," he said, gazing about him in admiration, "what a spiffing house. A fellow could have a good time playing hide-and-seek in here. Was old Wren really such a moneybags?"

"Sir Wilfred," she said firmly, "earned his fortune through hard work and spent wisely. He liked beautiful things."

Adrian was quite unabashed. "I say, you girls look fine as fivepence," he said to the twins. "Do you have all the men running after you? I expect so, though I can't think why they would bother. If I were free and did not have to attend that infernal prison house, I should spend all my time at Tattersall's and Newmarket, and I should find out all the mills and cockfights and such. Never mind the girls."

"Adrian, my lad, sit down," Tom said with uncharacteristic firmness. "I would not think that the girls would be mightily upset to be ignored by you, you know. If you fail to take an interest in any of your studies at school, what will you have to offer them except a lot of talk about horses and mills? Not the sort of talk that will make you the darling of the ladies."

Adrian sat. "You still scold as much as ever, Mr. Russell," he said, quite uncowed by the picture just painted of his womanless future. "I say, Felicity, could I have one of those scones? I have not had human food for an age, I swear."

"You poor dear," Laura said, picking up a plate for him. "Here, I shall give you a jam tart as well. This one, I think. It has more jam than the others."

Tom took it upon himself to keep Adrian entertained for much of the next day. He took the boy riding in the park and drove him to Tattersall's. In the afternoon he and Felicity took Adrian to the Tower of London and Astley's Circus. They stopped for ices on the way home. It had been a pleasant, carefree afternoon, Felicity decided, so unlike anything she had been used to with Wilfred. She had been somewhat alarmed the day before by Adrian's apparent lack of manners and indifference to education. But she had realized that he was merely a typical fifteen-year-old. His manners were open and frank but not, in fact, totally lacking. His disgust with his studies was largely a pose. As they traveled about London, and especially in the Tower itself, it became apparent that the boy did, in fact, possess a great deal of general knowledge about the city and about history. Knowledge and interest. He insisted on seeing everything in the Tower until Felicity felt that her feet would not support her much longer.

It was an afternoon that brought back memories of her own girlhood, for some reason. It was certainly not the surroundings that did this. The city of London in no way resembled the countryside in which she had grown up. It must have been their high spirits, she concluded. They all seemed to be laughing most of the time, though she could not remember afterward what had seemed so funny at the time. There was, of course, the moment when she and Tom had been quite sedately admiring the view from the parapets of the Tower and Adrian had come running up to them, declaring that it was time for Felicity to have a swim in the river. He had bent down, wrapped his arms around her legs, and pretended to heave upward. Tom had taken a firm hold of her arm and declared himself ready to help in the task of hurling her over the edge. Felicity had squealed and giggled just like a girl, and had continued helpless with laughter when Adrian, abandoning the original plan, snatched her straw bonnet from her head and dangled it over the parapet.

"Adrian!" she had shrieked. "That is a new bonnet. Oh, if you just knew how I searched and searched until I found just the right one. You horrid boy. Give it back at once."

"You had better do as you're told if you want any dinner," Tom advised. "She has a garret at the top of her house where she puts recalcitrant schoolboys until they repent, you know, Adrian."

"Oops!" Adrian said suddenly as the bonnet fell from his hand, and he slapped the other hand over his mouth. "I say, I am most awfully sorry, Felicity. What rotten bad luck."

Felicity squealed and leaned dangerously over the parapet in the expectation of seeing the ruins of her bonnet floating away on the Thames. Tom, helpless with laughter himself, grabbed her waist.

"Oh, you horrid boy!" she exclaimed. "Oh, I might have known!" She dissolved into giggles as Adrian hauled on the ribbon that was concealed in his palm and the bonnet came into view again.

"You see what I meant about your brother?" Tom said, laughing into her brimming eyes.

"Yes," she said, "and between the two of you, you have probably ruined my reputation for ladylike demeanor if anyone has seen us this afternoon. What an undignified spectacle we must present. Give me my bonnet at once, horrid boy. And you, sir, may remove your hands from my waist whenever you wish."

All quite ridiculous, quite juvenile and undignified, Felicity concluded after they had arrived home. And marvelous! She had quite forgotten what it was like just to have fun, not for any reason but that one enjoyed another's company. It had been sheer ill

fortune that had sent Lord Waite and Lady Dorothea
Page driving past Gunter's in an open carriage just
when the three of them were eating ices and laughing over some piece of nonsense. And what had
made him look and see them there? And why, oh,
why, had he decided to stop his carriage, hand the
ribbons to his tiger, and bring Lady Dorothea over to
them?

His intended looked so perfect, dressed all in ice
blue, her chin—and nose, it seemed—raised disdain-
fully. He looked impeccable, his dove-gray riding
coat and top hat proclaiming him every inch the
aristocrat. Felicity had to force her hands to stay
away from her head. She was convinced that her
bonnet must be askew and that several strands of
hair must have pulled loose from her coiffure during
the scuffle with Adrian. She smiled and introduced
Adrian and tried to behave as if she were sitting in
her own drawing room, fresh from her boudoir.

"You have ice cream on your chin, Felicity," Adrian
proclaimed to the world.

"Here, allow me," Tom said, turning to her as she
raised her hand. He pulled a handkerchief from his
pocket, leaned intimately toward her, and dabbed
gently at her chin. Having removed the offending
spot, he raised his eyes to hers and smiled that
devastating crinkle-eyed smile that quite made her
stomach do a little jump as she smiled back.

The incident lasted but a moment, but when Felicity looked back at her visitors, she saw a look of
disdain on the lady's face, one of a pale-eyed blank-
ness on the gentleman's. She really did not know
how he had reacted, but she was glad that Tom had
been quick enough to keep up the charade of their
intimacy. Though she could have wished the incident to be one of less embarrassment to herself. Ice
cream on her chin, indeed. And she Lady Felicity
Wren!

"Who are *they*?" Adrian asked, pulling a face as
soon as the pair had bowed and taken their leave.

"Gunter's should hire her. She could make the ices freeze with a glance. He is top-of-the-trees, though. Did you notice that cravat, Mr. Russell?"

"Yes," Tom said amiably, "I would imagine it took his valet all of two hours to perfect the creation, my lad."

They all felt quite hagged by the time Adrian was returned to school on Sunday evening after dinner. Cook was close to exhaustion, having spent her usually easy day making tarts, sconces, cream cakes, and muffins for the dear young lad to take back to the school with him. The "dear young lad" had haunted the kitchens whenever no other entertainment offered itself, shamelessly flattering the cook and bringing her close to tears when he described the spartan fare on which they existed at Eton. She felt it her duty as a compassionate human being to send enough food back with Adrian to feed not only him but all the other boys of his dormitory who had not been favored with a weekend of human living.

The twins too had allowed themselves to be worn ragged all of Sunday after church, doing whatever their brother wished to do. As Laura explained to Felicity later that evening, one could tell how repressed the poor boy's spirits were at school if he had so much energy to expend as soon as he was let loose. Tom, who was present at the time, refrained from asking what had caused the identical exuberance in the boy when he had been at home. He knew what the answer would be. Doubtless it would have been the boy's tutor who was to blame.

Felicity felt rather as if her head had been spinning on her shoulders for three days. Her brother was a veritable whirlwind. But she was pleased that he had come. He had brought back so many pleasant memories of what family life and simple friendship could be like. She had asked herself more than once in the last few days if she and Tom and Cedric had ever been such bundles of irrepressible energy as her youngest brother was now. And she had had to admit in sheer astonishment that they had. Tom had been almost sixteen when he—or Cedric—had pushed her into the stream. She had been fifteen, Tom seventeen when they had hidden in the branches of the oak tree one afternoon, quite silent, dropping acorns on the head of Miss Long, her governess, who was looking and calling in vain for her charge to come for her harpsichord lesson. They had almost fallen out of the tree when the poor lady had moved out of earshot, so uncontrollable were their snorts and giggles. How horridly they had behaved! How wonderful those days had been!

And had it not been for Adrian's visit, she might have forgotten forever those golden days. She had grown so far from that life in her days with Wilfred. And she had taken it for granted that she wished to move farther still into the life of elegance and frivolous gaiety of the *beau monde*. Of course, she still did. Unfortunately, one could never go back in life. One had continually to move forward to new things. She had moved too far from the world of Adrian and Tom to ever go back to it. She would be bored, surely she would, if life were always as it had been for the last three days, family-oriented, without one social engagement to add glitter to life. And she could never live permanently in the country again. How ever would she fill her days?

But she most not forget. And she must make sure that her children grew up in the country, where they could be carefree and boisterous if they wished without always being under the eye of reproving parents. Strange! She had never thought of having children with Lord Waite. She could not imagine him as a father. But she had always wanted children, had always considered that her life would not be complete without. It had been one of the trials of life with Wilfred as time and her youth slipped past, to know that she could not give birth as long as he lived on. She and Tom had wanted six children. She smiled, watching him down on the floor playing a game of pick-up sticks with Lucy. It would have been good. Six would have been no burden to him. He would have played with them all with the same patient cheerfulness that he displayed now. Felicity felt an instant's regret. She had assumed in the last month that Wilfred had rescued her from a life of dullness with Tom. But maybe it would not have been dull. Had she never moved away from home, never traveled, never sampled the delights of society, she might have been happy. She would always have been sure of Tom's devotion. She would have had several of his children by now. She wondered curiously if he ever felt similar regrets. She thought of asking him, but the question was too personal even for their friendship.

Each of the ladies in the house at Pall Mall peered anxiously from the windows when they arose on the morning of the garden party. The weather had been warm and sunny for so long that it seemed inevitable that rain and wind and coldness would return soon. All three were delighted to note that it would not be today. The sun shone yet again from a sky in which just a few lazy white puffs floated.

Lucy and Laura sat in the morning room whiling away the hours until they might begin to get ready. Lucy had a book open on her lap; Laura was stroking her chin with the feather of a pen. A blank sheet of paper lay before her on the desk. But neither was involved with her apparent task. They were deep in one of their conversations that would have sounded strange to a listener. They seemed much of the time to be indulging in two separate monologues, only occasionally sharing the same topic. Yet they listened to each other. Each one later knew exactly what the other had said and what the other had been feeling.

"It is four days since I have seen Darlington," Lucy was saying. "It seems longer. Is that a good sign or a bad?"

"After a while one stops meeting new people," Laura said, "and seems to associate with the same crowd. I seem to be coupled with Viscount Varley much of the time and I am not sure that I wish to be. It is just that there no longer seems to be any choice."

"I have a feeling that he is going to declare himself soon," Lucy continued, and it was obvious to both of them that she spoke of the earl, not of Varley. "I don't know why I think so. He has never said anything of a very personal nature, though he always singles me out when we are at the same function. But I believe he will propose. What if he does so today?"

"I really like him," Laura said. "He is very charming and one feels good to be with such a very handsome man. He is easily the best-looking man in London, is he not?"

"I just do not know how I shall respond," Lucy said. "Of course, to be a countess is a very dazzling prospect, and I am sure that he is a very worthy gentleman. But do I really wish to marry him?"

"But looks are not everything, are they?" Laura said. "And charm is not either, for all that it makes a man pleasant company. Is there anything beneath the charm? That is the question."

"It has been so easy, you see," Lucy continued. "No sparks. No challenge. Now, if someone could just be induced to insult me so that Darlington would fight a duel for me and maybe be horribly wounded and be at death's door, and I could nurse him back to health, for all everyone would say that it was most improper of me to be alone in his bedchamber so much, then I might accept his proposal without a shadow of doubt."

"And what if he should propose?" Laura asked. "Of course, I am not at all sure that his thoughts are bending that way. I think he may be a man who just enjoys dangling after a girl. He is only four-and-twenty, you know. Many men of his rank do not think of marriage until they are old and in their thirties."

"Like Lord Waite," said Lucy, unexpectedly joining her sister's thread of conversation. "I thought he would have offered for Felicity by now. Have you noticed the way he looks at her?"

"I believe Mr. Russell still has a *tendre* for her," Laura said. "Did you see them dancing at Almack's? They did not take their eyes from each other's face. I felt my face grow hot just to watch them."

"For all he has such light-blue eyes," Lucy continued, definitely not describing Tom, "they look as if they are on fire when he gazes at Felicity. And I believe she favors him, too. She always takes his white roses to her room, except for that one day when the girl who does our rooms told me she had thrown them out. They must have quarreled that time. It was the day after she went to Vauxhall with him. Maybe he dared to kiss her." She giggled.

"And he spends a great deal of time with us or with her," Laura said. "It is not quite natural when he is unmarried and really not *that* old. You would think he would be setting up a flirt. Unless he still carries a torch for Felicity, of course."

"Remember how we always used to cry over that story?" Lucy asked. "When Mama used to tell us how much in love they were, but Felicity was forced to marry our brother-in-law because he was rich and we were poor."

"We always cried at the part where she stole away from the house the night before the wedding," Laura said, "and everyone knew she was going to meet Mr. Russell, because he had come posthaste home, though no one said anything."

"We were only ten at the time," Lucy said, "and quite unaware. We only thought about how wonderful it was to have a sister getting married."

"Would it not be romantic," Laura sighed, "if they were to fall in love again and get married?"

"And we could be bridesmaids," Lucy said, "that

is, of course, if I am not married to Darlington by that time."

"What shall I do this afternoon?" Laura said. "Shall I try to meet someone new? Or would it be more comfortable to allow Varley to monopolize my time?"

"I wonder if he *will* ask this afternoon," Lucy said, the look in her eyes indicating that she was not thinking of Varley.

Felicity's mind too was preoccupied with the afternoon's engagement. There was nothing so extraordinary about the garden party except that it was being given by Laura's particular friends, the Townsends. But somehow Adrian's three-day visit had been a large breathing space in the hectic round of activities, and now it was almost like starting the Season all over again. It was four days since she had seen Lord Waite, if one discounted that brief and embarrassing meeting at Gunter's.

She wondered if she was anywhere near achieving her goal. Over the previous few weeks she had repeatedly encouraged him with smiles and acceptances of brief outings and dances. She had just as often repulsed him, claiming she was out when she was not, or otherwise engaged when he arrived to take her driving. And whenever she had been with Tom in his presence, the two of them had looked at each other and behaved as if there was more than mere friendship between them.

Lord Waite was as persistent as ever in his attentions. The roses came every morning. He called at the house most days. He always approached her, if only briefly, at every social gathering. But he had said nothing of a personal nature since his words at Almack's. And she had no idea how he was affected by her continuing flirtation with Tom. Sometimes he looked amused, as if he fully knew the truth of the matter. At other times his face was expressionless and she did not know what he thought. But she did know that as far as his understanding with Lady Dorothea was concerned, the feelings of neither were engaged. There was nothing but a massive boredom in evidence when the two were together. Felicity could feel no guilt about trying to steal him away from his intended bride.

And steal him she would. Today was the start of a new week, the weather was delightful, and of all entertainments she loved a garden party best. Today she must make a push to bring about her desire. She looked again at the pale-lemon sprigged-muslin dress that already lay on the bed. Was it the dress in which to win the campaign, with the straw bonnet that Adrian had pretended to drop from the Tower of London? Was it too insipid with her gold hair? Felicity smiled. I am behaving more and more like a girl these days, she thought.

✄ 10 ✄

The grounds of the Townsend mansion were ide-
ally suited to a garden party. Indeed, it was an
annual event, Laura discovered later, much enjoyed
by the *ton*, though this was the first year that Lady
Pamela had been allowed to attend. During previous
years she had had to watch the proceedings from
the windows of a room opposite the schoolroom, in
company with her governess.

Lawns stretched from the house almost as far as
the eye could see. But there was no chance of mo-
notony. Trees shaded guests from the glare of the
sun, numerous flower beds, fountains, statues, and
flower-decked trellises pleased the eye, adding color
and fragrance to the afternoon. Two long hothouses,
the pride and joy of Lady Townsend and her gardener, were open for the delight and admiration of
the visitors. An octagonal summer house, its walls
within lined with green velvet-covered benches, was
far from the house among shady trees but provided
comfortable relaxation for anyone who felt inclined
to stroll that far.

The lawn closest to the house was lined with tables covered with crisp linen cloths and laden with
refreshments of all kinds. By the time Lady Wren
arrived with her escort, Mr. Russell, and her twin
sisters, the same lawn was already crowded with
chattering groups of people, most with a plate or

glass in hand. Lady Pamela immediately whisked away the twins, an arm linked through each of theirs.

"Mr. Sotheby, my cousin, wishes to meet you," she said. "He arrived in town but yesterday and is eager to see these twins whom very few people can tell apart."

"May I get you some lemonade, Flick?" Tom suggested, and he pushed his way past a crowd toward a footman who was circulating with a large tray of drinks.

"I am so pleased you were able to come, Lady Wren," Lady Townsend said at her elbow. "Pamela is very fond of your sisters, especially Laura. They are nicely behaved girls, though I do wish I could tell them apart when they are together. Now, which of them is wearing peach and which pink?"

Felicity laughed. "I think perhaps we should have their names embroidered across the back of each garment," she said. "But then they would probably deliberately exchange clothes. Trying to confuse people about their identities is a favorite game with them, I'm afraid. Lucy is peach today; Laura, pink."

"Well, they look remarkably pretty, anyway," her companion said, "and very good for Pamela. She has always been such a shy girl. And now look at her."

The three girls were sitting on the grass under a tree, five gentlemen paying court to them. Felicity noticed that two of those men—the one leaning indolently against the tree trunk and the one reclining on the grass, propped on one elbow—were the Earl of Darlington and Viscount Varley.

"Lady Townsend, I do adore your gardens. Mama has always said that she would steal away your gardener if she thought her reputation could survive the theft." The speaker was Lady Dorothea Page, looking quite lovely in a white muslin gown trimmed with royal-blue ribbons, her bonnet and parasol matching the ribbons exactly. One of her hands rested on the arm of Lord Waite.

"Indeed, ma'am," he added, "you must have been quite punctilious in your prayers recently to have been granted such a perfect day."

Lady Townsend tittered and said all that was proper before wafting away to greet some other newly arrived guests.

"All alone, Lady Wren?" Lord Waite asked, eyebrows raised. "We have a poor-spirited crop of gentlemen this Season if you are left for so long."

"No, indeed, my lord," Felicity assured him with her half-smile. "Tom has merely gone in pursuit of some lemonade for me. I see he has been delayed by Miss Peignton and her mama."

"I do compliment you on your bonnet, Lady Wren," Lady Dorothea said languidly. "I have searched for just such an one."

Felicity was just beginning to wonder how she was to sustain a conversation with these two when Tom returned and handed her a glass. "I am sorry to have been so long, my love," he said before turning to acknowledge the presence of her two companions, "but I see that you have not been left alone. Waite? Lady Page? How d'ye do?"

Viscount Varley had succeeded in separating Laura from her companions. They were walking very slowly around the edge of the garden, examining the flower beds and the shrubbery. Laura, twirling her pink parasol gaily, was reflecting on the fact that he had singled her out even before the earl had paid particular attention to Lucy. It seemed that he had finally learned to distinguish one from the other. But she would put the matter to the test, anyway.

"I wonder if you know with which twin you are walking, my lord," she said archly.

He looked at her, his handsome eyebrows arched above his eyes, then smiled his very white-toothed smile. "Ah, you seek to tease me, as always," he said. "For a while, I must admit, you and your sister had me mystified. You are extraordinarily alike. How-

ever, I have discovered that knowing you are Laura
is really quite simple. You are by far the lovelier of
the two, you see."

Laura blushed and twirled the handle of her parasol. "And if I were to tell you now that I am Lucy?"
she asked.

He laughed. "I should hate to have to contradict a
lady," he said, "but I should call you a liar."

"Oh," she said, and the parasol twirled wildly
behind her head.

The viscount took one of her hands and tucked it
beneath his arm. "I have traveled widely," he said
with his charming smile, "and have known ladies in
all the main cities of Europe—Paris, Vienna, Brussels—
but I have never met one prettier than you, Laura.
May I call you that? Especially by daylight. Many
women bear up well enough under candlelight. Most
appear sallow or pockmarked in the light of the sun.
Your complexion is flawless and so delicate." They
had stopped walking. He flicked the backs of the
fingers of his free hand across one of her cheeks. "I
should dearly love to kiss you, but I am afraid we
are in full view of at least two hundred people."

Laura blushed deeply. "And very thankful I am,
too," she said. "I do not believe a kiss should be
carelessly given. I have never been kissed."

"Careless!" he said, his eyes roaming her face. He
turned and began to walk again, her arm still linked
with his. "I am sorry you think I spoke with levity,
Laura. I mean honorably. I would not wish to kiss
you if I did not also wish to make you my wife."

Laura was the one to stop this time. "You want to
marry me?" she asked, eyes wide.

"But of course." He favored her with the full force
of his smile. "I must marry eventually. It is one of
the disadvantages of bearing a title that one must
perform the duty of perpetuating one's line. I have a
comfortable fortune so I need not marry money. I
am free to choose the loveliest lady I can find. To-

gether you and I will dazzle society, Laura. You
have but to say yes."

Laura stood looking up at this very handsome
face, waiting, she supposed, for more. She had been
complimented highly by the most gorgeous man in
London, proposed to by him. She should be ecstatic.
Was something missing? She could not think what it
could be. As he had just said, all she had to do was
say yes. She must be stunned, she decided.

He smiled and leaned toward her. "I have taken
you by surprise, I see," he said. "You expected me
to take longer to come to the point? Or did you not
think I would be free to choose below my own titled
ranks? I have chosen you, Laura, and when I make
up my mind to something, I am all impatient haste
to have the matter settled. You will find that that is
one of my characteristics. Can you give me an answer now, or do you need time?"

"I am very sensible of the honor you have done
me, my lord," she said, "but as you say, I have been
taken by surprise. I beg you will give me a little
time."

He raised her hand to his lips, looking into her
eyes the whole time. "A week perhaps, Laura," he
said. "I am not a patient man. You will give me your
answer then?"

"Yes," she said faintly.

He tucked her hand through his arm again and
began to walk back in the direction of the house and
the refreshments.

Lucy and Lady Pamela were still sitting under the
tree surrounded by a small group of men. The Earl
of Darlington still leaned indolently against the trunk
behind Lucy, so that she could not see or converse
with him without deliberately turning her head and
her body. She waited in some puzzlement for him to
join her on the grass or participate more fully in the
animated conversation going on around them or offer to bring her some food or drink. He did none of
these things but stood in silence.

Finally Lady Pamela's frequent escort, Mr. Booth, suggested escorting her to the hothouses so that she might identify for him all the exotic blooms that he had heard of. Mr. Sotheby bowed to Lucy and asked if she would like to join them. She was quiet for a moment, waiting for some reaction from the man behind her. There was none. She smiled at Pamela's cousin, who stood so anxiously before her, placed her hand on his, and allowed him to draw her to her feet. She still delayed, opening her peach parasol with great care, and then she set out in the direction of the hothouses with her three companions.

It was much later in the afternoon when Lucy saw the earl again. He was coming out of the house with Lord Townsend and a group of other gentlemen. They must have been playing cards or billiards, she guessed. The earl had certainly not been in the garden during the hour or so since she had left the hothouses. She felt a vague unease. It was not at all like him to ignore her so completely. As she was thinking that, she caught his eye across the heads of several seated groups. He bowed his head in acknowledgment of her presence and began to thread his way past chairs and tables toward her.

"May I offer to fetch you something, Miss Maynard?" he asked politely. "Or find you a chair, perhaps?"

"No, thank you, my lord," she said. "I have been sitting most of the afternoon. And I just had tea."

There was an uncomfortable pause. "Would you care to walk?" he asked, extending an arm.

She took the arm and they began to walk away from the house and the crush of people. "It has been a splendid afternoon, has it not?" she asked, her voice sounding a trifle bleak.

"Yes, indeed," he said. "Lady Townsend has outdone herself on this occasion. Last year it rained, I believe, though that was not, of course, her fault."

Again silence. "The hothouses are quite magnificent," she said. "Have you seen them, my lord?"

"Yes," he replied, "last year while it rained."

Silence. Lucy wanted desperately to ask him what was wrong. Usually he was the one to initiate conversation. He had a pleasant easy manner that usually set her utterly at her ease. Now he was clearly not enjoying himself, had clearly not wanted to walk with her. She removed her hand from his arm. "I must go back, my lord," she said. "I promised Laura that I would join her soon. She will be looking for me."

He looked at her, frowning. "I shall be going away tomorrow," he said.

"Away? Tomorrow?" she echoed.

"I have to return home," he said. "My mother is unwell and I must satisfy myself that she is not seriously ill."

"Of course," Lucy said. "I am sorry. You do not know how long you will be away?"

"No," he said abruptly. "No, I do not know."

They approached the house in silence. Laura, it soon became apparent, was in the midst of a noisy, chattering group of young people. Darlington directed his companion toward them, but did not join the group.

"I hope we will meet again, Miss Maynard," he said. "I wish you all success in the remainder of the Season."

"Thank you," she said. "I hope you find your mother recovered, my lord."

He bowed, looked unsmilingly into her eyes for a moment, and was gone.

Lucy felt a sick emptiness in her stomach as she turned to join her twin and their acquaintances on the terrace. That was it, then? No more? Surely more should have been said than that, some sort of personal message of regret?

Lady Dorothea Page had drawn her escort away after a few minutes' polite conversation with Felicity and Tom.

"I fail to see how Lady Wren acquired her reputation for great beauty," Lady Dorothea said as they moved out of earshot. "If you were to ask me, I should say she looks quite insipid this afternoon. A yellow dress is hardly the garment to complement that yellow hair."

"I am sure you are right, my love," Lord Waite replied in his most bored manner. "However, in my opinion, pale lemon looks simply stunning with golden hair."

Felicity and Tom mingled with the crowd for the next hour and felt quite free to be themselves. Only later did Tom suggest that they take a stroll.

"I find it a strain to talk and talk about nothing at all," he said, taking a deep and grateful breath of fresh air laden with the fragrance of flowers. "Don't you, Flick?"

"But this is life, Tom," she said with a little laugh. "These are the people who matter. What if the talk is mainly of fashion and gossip? It is entertaining if one has a sense of humor. Is it so much duller than talking about sheep and crops all the time?"

He looked at her curiously. "I believe you are trying to set me down," he said, "but it will not serve, you know. I am not the bore you are hinting at, Flick. When did I ever talk about sheep and crops except in passing or with my bailiff or another man when there were no ladies to be bored? You wrong me. We always found plenty to talk about without having to gossip about other people or talk on mere trivialities constantly."

She looked back at him and bit her lip. "I am sorry, Tom," she said. "You are right, of course. But you and I were always an exceptional case, you see. For some reason we have always found it easy to talk to each other without any forethought. It is not that simple with most people. With most, if one waited for something worthwhile to say, there would be a universal silence."

"I do not understand you," Tom said. "This is the

life you want, where your intelligence and reading and sensitivity will be wasted? Are you sure that you will be happy?"

She laughed and squeezed his arm. "Tom," she said, "reading and conversing sensibly do not bring much excitement to life, you know. There are places enough to go and people enough to meet and occasions enough to attend to fill a lifetime with activity. Why question the usefulness of such a life if one is enjoying it? Is life of any use anyway, no matter how it is lived?"

Tom's pace slowed and he looked at her somewhat sadly. "I had not thought you so cynical, Flick," he said. "Have you enjoyed your weeks here so far? I mean, enough to make you feel that this is the way you wish to spend your life?"

"Of course not, silly," she said affectionately. "I am not married yet. When I am, Tom, to the right man, then life will be idyllic. No more dullness or boredom or uncertainty."

Tom glanced across at her and then ahead. Did she know how naive her expectations were? he wondered. Did she really believe that she had only to make an advantageous marriage to live happily ever after? He felt an almost overwhelming urge to stop and hug her to him, to swear to her that he would protect her from all the things that might prevent her enjoyment of life. Just as naive an attitude, he thought ruefully.

Then suddenly he did stop. Without even realizing it, they had walked almost as far as the summer house and Tom had just become aware that two people were inside, sitting side by side but not touching. He recognized the blue bonnet as that of Lady Page. Her companion was undoubtedly Lord Waite. They were facing Tom and Felicity. Tom glanced hastily back toward the house. It was almost out of sight behind some shady trees.

"Flick," he said, "are you still set on having Waite?"

"Oh, yes," she said. "I cannot give up on that goal now. My very pride depends on success."

"Then don't panic and smack my face," he said. "You are about to be kissed, my love, by a very ardent lover. Your man is facing this way in the summer house but will not know that we have seen him."

Felicity had no time either to glance toward the little structure or to offer an opinion on Tom's plan. She was pulled against him by very firm hands, one behind her waist and one around her shoulders. And then, even as she gasped in shock, Tom's mouth was on hers, not at all friendly or gentle. It was a lover's kiss, as he had promised, and Felicity responded immediately in kind. There had been no time to prepare herself, no time to wonder what it would be like to kiss Tom again after eight years. And there was no thought, as her body fit itself to his and her arms went around him and her head angled until her mouth opened beneath the warm seal of his, about how she would behave, how she could best arouse the jealousy of the man in the summer house. She abandoned herself, without thought or will, to the pleasurable ache of pure physical longing.

Nestled against Tom, from mouth to thighs, Felicity forgot that she was Lady Wren and he Thomas Russell, friend; she forgot the garden party, the presence close by of a few hundred of the most elite members of the *ton*; she forgot Lord Waite and Lady Page in the summer house; she forgot there *was* a Lord Waite. She knew only for a few moments that she was home at last.

Tom ended the kiss. He pressed her forehead firmly against his shoulder and held her there for a full minute. He was smiling rather wickedly when he finally allowed her to lift her head. "That should do it nicely," he said. "Don't look now, Flick, but they are still there. If I could look more pointedly, I'll wager I would find Waite's eyes even greener than the grass."

"Tom, you rogue," Felicity said, stifling a giggle, "that was *most* improper. In fact, I believe my honor dictates that you offer for me at once."

He lifted her hand and bent over it with mock reverence. "Ma'am," he said, "will you do me the great honor of becoming my wife?"

"Indeed, sir," she said, free hand over her heart, "I thought you would never ask. The honor would be all mine. And really, Tom, that is a splendid idea. Did you mean it? As part of the charade, I mean? How clever you are! Yes, of course, we must become betrothed. Where shall we make the announcement?" She linked her arm through his and turned purposefully in the direcion of the house again. "You are sure Lord Waite noticed, Tom? Oh, you wicked man. You kiss most awfully well, you know. Much better than he does." She giggled.

"I wish to be taken home immediately," Lady Dorothea was saying inside the summer house, her normally pale face flushed with indignation. "I have never been exposed to such a disgustingly vulgar display in my whole life. Lady Wren is no lady; she is no better than a light-skirts. And to flaunt her lover so publicly! I shall lie down at home and hope that I am sufficiently restored by dinnertime that Mama and Papa will not be alarmed for my health."

Lord Waite rose slowly to his feet. "Come, come, my love," he said, "you must have some fortitude. They were not so indiscreet after all. They were out of sight of the house and apparently did not know that we were witnesses to the whole embrace. These things happen between men and women, you know."

"I hope you would never dream of manhandling me so," Lady Dorothea said, fixing him with a steely glance. "I should not stand for such vulgarity, Edmond."

"Have no fear, my love," Waite replied evenly,

regarding her coolly from pale eyes. "I would never so much as think of touching you so."

Fortunately for him, Lady Dorothea made a close companion of her indignation during the walk back up the lawns. He did not have to make conversation. Lord Waite was perplexed, to say the least. He was not quite sure whether he was angry or disgusted. He knew one thing, though: he was no longer amused. He did not think they had seen him. The embrace, he was sure, was quite spontaneous. They had thought themselves unobserved. So he could not shrug off the incident as an act put on for his benefit. And he could no longer assure himself that the ardor was all on the side of Russell. She had responded to him with an eagerness that had not been feigned.

Waite felt that for once in his life he had badly miscalculated where a woman was concerned. He knew that she liked him, that she was attracted to him, that she wanted to be bedded by him. In his experience the women who desired him wanted him exclusively. He had assumed that Lady Wren was one of their number. He had set himself to playing the game with her, slowly if need be, confident in the assurance that sooner or later she would capitulate and be his for the taking until he had had his fill of her and was free to turn his fancies elsewhere again. But it seemed she was not so single-minded. While delaying the consummation with him, she had taken another lover. Waite had little doubt that those two had been to bed together. Russell's hands had stayed above her waist, but she had arched her whole body against him in a manner that suggested familiarity. Her hand had gone to his hair, and the angle of their heads had suggested a very deep kiss.

But why? What did she see in the other man? He was passable, Waite supposed with some disdain, but surely with no qualities of person or manner to recommend him to such an exquisite beauty as Lady

Wren. Why did she dally with Russell when she could have him?

Lord Waite, handing his intended into her carriage a few minutes later and seating himself across from her, decided that it was high time he and Felicity Wren had a confrontation. He did not mind a game of dalliance. He could even enjoy the spice it added to the acquisition of a new mistress. But he would not be made a fool of, and he would not share her. By God, he would not share her. She was his.

Felicity had much to occupy her thoughts during the coming evening and the following morning. Even so, she could not miss the pensive mood of both her sisters. They had looked forward with such enthusiasm to the garden party and it had seemed each time she had looked for them during the afternoon that they were well-occupied. She would have expected them to be exuberant, bubbling over with stories of how they had spent their time. Instead, they were both unusually quiet. Dinner was almost a strained occasion. Tom had excused himself and the three sisters dined alone, Felicity bearing the brunt of keeping the conversation alive.

She would have liked to creep away to her own room during the evening to try to sort out her own thoughts, but she really felt duty-bound first to see to the welfare of her sisters. She had taken on the responsibility of their come-out, but sometimes she felt that she was being sadly neglectful. She supposed that the practice of having a mother or grandmother or older aunt bringing out a young girl was, after all, a good idea. Such chaperones undoubtedly had nothing on their minds but the task at hand. They certainly did not have the added preoccupation of trying to settle themselves into an advantageous marriage.

Felicity found Lucy in the book room, an unusual

sanctuary for that particular twin. She had drawn a book from a shelf, but it lay unopened on her lap. Felicity, glancing at the cover, thought that the girl must be very distracted indeed to have selected a book of sermons that even Wilfred had probably never read. But then Wifred had always purchased books as he would pictures or vases: because they would increase the appearance of gentility that he cultivated.

"I have been looking for you, love," she said gently, seating herself opposite Lucy and resting her elbows on the arms of the chair. "May I be of any assistance to you?"

"What?" Lucy said. "Oh, no, thank you, Felicity. I have found what I want." She indicated the book in her lap.

"Did you enjoy yourself this afternoon?"

"Oh, yes," the girl said brightly. "Did you meet Mr. Sotheby, Pamela's cousin? He is very agreeable. He took me to see the hothouses."

"Yes," Felicity said, "he seems a personable young man. I believe I saw you walking with the Earl of Darlington, too, did I not?"

"Who?" said Lucy. "Oh, Darlington. Yes. He walked with me for a few minutes. He is going away, you know."

"Indeed?"

"Yes. His mama is indisposed. He has to go into the country."

"Oh? When does he return?" Felicity asked. "You will miss him."

"Who? Me?" said Lucy. "Gracious, no. I am enjoying myself too much to miss anyone. Oh, Felicity, he would not say when he will return. He hinted that he might not come back at all. I believe he was saying good-bye to me."

Felicity frowned. "And he matters to you, does he not?" she said. "And I am not surprised. He did seem very particular in his attentions. Is this why you are unhappy, love?"

Lucy flung down the book on the table beside her and jumped to her feet. "He was so strange, Felicity, so distant. It was not at all as if he had danced with me, paid calls on me, sent me flowers."

"Do you love him, Lucy?"

The girl sat down again and spread her hands on her lap. "I really do not know," she said. "Sometimes I think I might. But he is the only man who has really paid attention to me and he is an attractive man and he is an earl. I don't know if I am just flattered and dazzled or if I really care for him. But I need not puzzle over the matter any longer, need I? He made his own sentiments very clear this afternoon. I am hurt, that is all. But you need not worry for me. Mr. Sotheby has asked for the first dance and the supper dance at the Grayson ball tomorrow evening and Mr. Pendleton has reserved the second dance."

Felicity felt concern for her sister and a degree of anger against the earl. It was true that he had not compromised Lucy in any way, and as far as she knew, he had never indicated that he meant matrimony. Yet his marked attentions to the girl at every function they attended and the frequency with which he had called on her and invited her to drive had surely set many people to speculating and had understandably raised the girl's expectations. He had seemed a gentleman; Felicity had liked him. She was disappointed in him.

She found Laura in the music room, playing only indifferently well on the spinet. Her mind was clearly not on the tune that she was trying to reproduce.

"Do you need the music?" Felicity asked. "It is in the stool, you know."

"Oh, no," Laura replied airily, "I really do not wish to play. I cannot settle to anything. I have just begun three letters to Mama and have torn them all up. When I sought out Lucy, she merely growled at me. We must all be tired."

"It would be hardly surprising," her sister agreed.

"I do not know when we last had a decently early night. Did you enjoy the garden party, Laura?"

"Rather," the girl replied. "Do you know what happened, Felicity? You would never guess in a million years. I was never more surprised in my life, though I have wondered, of course."

Felicity laughed. "Since I do not have a million years to spare," she said, "suppose you tell me."

"Varley offered for me!" Laura announced, saucer-eyed. "Can you imagine? For me!"

"Is this true?" Felicity asked. "I must confess I had not thought the viscount to be in the marriage market."

"He says he must marry sometime," Laura said, "and he said that I am prettier than any other girl he has ever met." She giggled. "Including Lucy. Can you imagine anything more absurd? We are identical."

Felicity frowned. "Did you accept him, Laura? Do you love him?"

Laura giggled again. "I do not know," she said. "He is most awfully handsome. I turn a little weak at the knees every time I look at him. And he is a viscount, Felicity, and wealthy, I believe. Just imagine, I could be a countess and have several homes and all sorts of money at my disposal."

"Those things are not everything," Felicity said. "Happiness is the most important thing. You must be sure that you could be happy with the viscount, that you would deal together well in friendship." She frowned again as she heard the words that were coming from her mouth.

"Oh, yes, I know," Laura said, "I know. I have a week in which to decide. I really do not know what to do, Felicity."

"Has he said anything about going to talk to Papa?" Felicity asked.

"No," Laura said. "I suppose he wants to be sure of my answer first."

Altogether, Felicity thought as she retired to bed that night, life was becoming somewhat complicated for all three of them. One of them had been rejected by a man who had seemed almost sure to propose; one had received an offer from a man who had seemed a mere dallier; and one had just betrothed herself to one man in the hope of winning an offer from another. She sighed as she drew a brush through her long golden hair, now loosened around her shoulders. They had, after all, to put the matter quite bluntly, come to London husband-hunting. They could not expect the matter to be without its problems and decisions and heartaches. And what of her own case? Was she any closer to winning Lord Waite than she had ever been? It was true that the white roses still came each morning and that he called most afternoons, frequently when she was from home. But she had had no private talk with him for several days. This afternoon, apart from the few moments of stilted conversation on the terrace when they had first arrived, he had made no effort to single her out. Of course, to be fair, it had not been an auspicious occasion on which to do so. Lady Dorothea had not left his side, and she had been with Tom most of the time.

But she had to wonder if he was still interested in her and if she was doing the right thing to try to incur his jealousy. What if her flirtation with Tom was driving him away from her rather than bringing him closer? That kiss especially, about which she was not prepared to think too closely at the moment, might well have given him a disgust of her. And she wanted him so badly. More and more when she saw him, she would picture herself at his side. His tall, elegant figure was so undoubtedly aristocratic. As his wife, she would be at the very heart of the *ton*, accepted unquestioningly wherever she went, deferred to as one of London's leading hostesses. She would never again be looked at askance, pitied even, as she had been, she was sure, as Wilfred's wife. Yes, she still wanted him. And she must make him see that he wanted her badly enough to offer her marriage. She had no doubt that once married to him, she would be able to keep him. She had looks and charms that he admired, she knew. She would spend her time making sure that she pleased and satisfied him so that he would never feel the need to take a mistress again. It would be a small price to pay for all that she would gain in exchange. He was, after all, a very attractive man. She would enjoy his attentions. She might even grow to love him.

If only Lord Waite were her sole problem! Felicity sighed. There was Tom, too. She was very much aware that she had stretched the bounds of their friendship quite outrageously. Perhaps too far. She was certainly making more and more demands on him as time passed. At first it was to be a mild flirtation to arouse jealousy. Now she was demanding that they become betrothed. Her trouble, she decided, was that she was by far too impulsive. Requesting Tom to go through a mock engagement with her was far more serious than suggesting a mere flirtation. If the betrothal were to seem convincing, then only she and Tom must be aware that it was not real. They had already decided that, in fact. But that meant that the twins must believe the engagement real, and it was too much to expect that Laura would not immediately dash off letters to Mama and Papa, to Cedric, and to Adrian. Mama would spread the news at home.

She had really done something unforgivable. Tom had, of course, agreed to the scheme. He was too good-natured ever to put up a fight if he thought he was helping her. But she was going to have to put him through dreadful embarrassment when it came time to cry off so that she might marry Lord Waite. He would be the jilted lover, the laughingstock, perhaps. At home he would be pitied. Poor, dear Tom. How could she do this to him? It was still not too late to put a stop to the matter, she supposed. Tom, taking charge of the situation once she had initiated it, had decided that the announcement must go into the *Morning Post* immediately. He would see to it. If she sent a message right now. . . .

Felicity went to stand by the window of her bed-chamber. She pulled back the heavy curtains and gazed out onto a garden faintly lit by moonlight. That kiss! She had tried not to think about it all evening, but it kept nagging at the edges of her mind. It had merely been a part of their playacting, staged for the benefit of one of the watchers in the summer house. It had been no more than that.

The trouble was, though, that it had been a great deal more than that. There was no doubt about it, when one faced the matter honestly, that it had been a very real kiss—on her part, anyway. She had not thought of Tom in that way for many years. Her love for him as a friend had survived very strongly, but she had assumed that the physical passion that had developed in the year before she married Wilfred had died with her youth. It had been just a bittersweet part of her growing up. She had touched him many times since their reunion. She had even hugged him at the first meeting. And he had always been just Tom. Despite the touches, he had remained one person and she another.

What had happened that afternoon, then? When his lips had met hers, she could no more have stopped her response than she could have stopped breathing. He had become within her arms that missing part of her life, the very air she breathed. If he had not kept his head, she thought, cheeks burning, she would have been begging and begging him to take her, as she had on that other dreadful night. But she had been just a naive girl, then, too young to have learned to control her own emotions. It was most alarming to know that it could happen again.

She could not start feeling for Tom again that way. It would be totally unrealistic to start thinking of him in terms of matrimony. They would never suit. He could not live long away from home; she could not rusticate. Anyway, far more important, she could not burden Tom with an unwelcome love. He was so fond of her, so good to her, that he would probably agree to marry her just to make her happy. The thought did not bear contemplation. Poor Tom: trapped first into a flirtation, then into betrothal, and finally into marriage. And Felicity was finally beginning to believe him when he said that all he wanted was his quiet bachelor existence.

No, she must be very careful. It was a thorough nuisance to have discovered that Tom still had the power to stir her blood. She did not want to have those feelings for him and she must be very careful to make sure that he never had so much as a hint of the fact. He was doing so much for her already.

Lord Waite had decided on a bold step. He could try to get Lady Wren alone at the Grayson ball. But it was so deucedly difficult with Dorothea and her mama forever hovering over him and with that troublesome country squire forever dogging Felicity's footsteps. If he visited her that afternoon, the chances were that she would be out or that there would be several other visitors in the drawing room. And by the time he asked her to drive out with him, someone would have forestalled him or she would pretend to a previous engagement merely to tease him.

He sent a footman in the morning with a note asking if she would drive out with him early in the afternoon, to Richmond. He added that he wished particularly to speak with her. The footman was to await an answer. The footman, as it happened, had time for several cakes and two mugs of ale in the kitchen before carrying a letter of acceptance back to his master. Lady Wren and her sisters were out shopping when he arrived.

Lord Waite's letter had, of course, been calculated to draw acceptance from Felicity. She was intrigued to know what the particularly important communication was to be. Had that embrace yesterday accomplished its aim so successfully? Was he about to offer for her? She chose her clothes with care and greeted him in the hallway a vision of loveliness in an apricot muslin dress, a russet pelisse and parasol, and her straw bonnet, which had new russet ribbons threaded through it in addition to the yellow.

"Ah, quite beautiful, my lady," he said, bowing in courtly manner over her hand.

It soon became evident to Felicity, as he threaded his team with practiced skill through the heavy traffic of the streets, that they were not headed for Richmond. He had been keeping up a steady stream of light, distracting conversation.

"Where are we going, my lord?" she asked.

He broke his concentration on the road long enough to turn and smile at her. "Now that I finally have you to myself for a few hours, Felicity," he said, "I intend to be alone with you."

She felt a twinge of alarm. "Oh?" she said in her most cool and aloof voice. "And am I permitted to know where we are to be alone together, my lord?"

"I told you once before of a house I possess," he said. "We are going there. My staff is expecting us. And my name is Edmond, remember?"

"I would prefer to remain in the open air," she said, twirling her parasol with apparent unconcern. "One day soon this weather will break. It is such a shame to miss the sunshine."

He laughed. "You are a born tease, Felicity," he said, "but today it will not work. You and I have some talking to do."

There was nothing for it but to twirl the parasol and gaze nonchalantly around her as if it were an everyday occurrence to be abducted to the house where a man kept his mistresses. She was certainly not going to show any sign of fear or other indication that she was naive and inexperienced.

Felicity gazed furtively around her when her companion finally drew the curricle to a halt. It was a quiet, perfectly respectable-looking neighborhood. She had half-expected troops of prostitutes to be strutting up and down displaying their wares. Lord Waite had jumped down from his place and handed the ribbons to a groom who had appeared from the side of the house.

"You need not look so tense, Felicity," he said, perfectly reading her thoughts. "Everything is quite genteel, as you see."

The butler seemed to be a perfect pillar of propriety. He bowed as he took his master's hat and whip, bowed as he took Felicity's bonnet and pelisse, bowed again as Waite handed him his coat. And having handed all these offerings to a lesser mortal, he led the way, stiff-backed, up a narrow staircase with ornate banister, opened the doors of a drawing room, stood to one side, and bowed again.

"Will that be all, m'lord," he asked.

"I shall ring," Lord Waite said, eyes on Felicity, and the butler closed the doors. Felicity wondered how deaf those respectable ears would be if she should see fit to scream within the next hour. She stood in the middle of the room and donned her mask of aloofness.

"Well, Edmond," she said, "you have me alone. And now perhaps you can relieve my curiosity and tell me what is of such importance that Richmond would not do at all."

He laughed and shrugged himself out of his coat of blue superfine. One part of Felicity's mind wondered curiously how he would get himself back inside it later. So close-fitting was it, so perfectly molded to his figure, that it must have taken a very determined and muscular valet to help him into it earlier. She deliberately let her eyes wander lazily over his white silk shirt with its lace-edged sleeves, the high cravat, the neckcloth tied into its usual intricate folds. She raised her eyebrows and looked inquiringly into his eyes.

"Come here, Felicity," he said "and be kissed. I

want to see if I can do better than your country swain."

"I beg your pardon?" she said, all haughty innocence.

"You did not know that you were observed, did you?" he said. "Yesterday at the garden party, I mean."

"With Tom?" she said, biting her lower lip. "You saw?"

"And was not greatly delighted," he assured her. "Will you be pleased to know that I was jealous, Felicity? Horribly jealous. He is not for you, you know. You are far too exquisite a creature to be thrown away on such as he. 'Caviar to the general,' as the immortal bard once said."

He had walked toward her as he spoke, and stopped now, not a foot away. One long, slim finger traced the line of her jaw from ear to chin and remained there while his thumb traced her lips. "You are meant for me, Felicity," he said. "You know that, do you not? I shall make love to you shortly and at the end of it you will admit to me that no man will ever again mean as much to you."

Felicity gazed into his eyes. She was not yet afraid, though he had just made perfectly clear what he intended to do with her before they left the house. This was the man she intended to marry. She was curious to feel his touch, anxious to find that he could affect her as Tom had done the day before. So she waited for his kiss. She would think a little later of how to avoid greater intimacies.

He did not oblige her immediately. He placed both hands on her shoulders and allowed them to wander downward, exploring her body as if it were naked before him. She stood perfectly still, too shocked to move and not really knowing how she should react. He stroked her breasts with light fingers and cupped their fullness in his palms, circling the tips with his thumbs. He traced the slim curve of her waist, the feminine curves of her hips, the out-

line of her legs, the softness of her inner thighs. It
was an unnerving exploration, made more so by the
fact that his eyes followed his hands through the
whole journey.

Felicity felt an uncomfortable heat spreading up
her spine and into her face. Her breathing quick-
ened. He smiled into her eyes and kissed her. She
was not allowed to fit herself to the embrace as she
had with Tom. One very determined hand had gone
behind her hips and pressed her against him so that
she was left in no doubt at all about the state of his
feelings. The other hand was twined painfully into
her tightly pinned chignon. She was totally at his
mercy. The sheer demand of his mouth had opened
hers and made her helpless against the invasion of
his tongue. She tried to relax, tried to remind herself
that this was her chosen husband, the man to whom
she was willing to surrender the right to her body.
She tried to enjoy, to feel desire and excitement
rather than building panic.

Then she was pushing blindly, mindlessly against
his chest, shaking her head violently from side to
side, gasping and clawing. And then, finding herself
blessedly free, she smacked him with a satisfying
crack across the side of the head.

"Why, you little bitch," he exclaimed, one hand
flying to cover his wounded cheek.

"My lord," she gasped, bosom heaving, eyes flash-
ing, "no one takes such liberties with my person
without my express permission. How dare you, sir!
How can you call yourself a gentleman?"

His lips had thinned. His pale eyes were arctic as
they looked back directly into hers. "What is it you
do want, ma'am?" he asked. "I have made it clear
from the start what I want from you. I assumed you
desired the same. You are no girl, no virgin, to be so
nice in your scruples. You must have realized when
you entered this house with me that you were
consenting to make love with me."

"It seems to me, my lord, that I was given no choice," she said coolly.

"Oh, come, come, Felicity," he said impatiently, "do not overdramatize your situation. Were you tied and gagged?"

"I did not give my consent, sir," she said.

"What is it you want?" he asked. "You are a wealthy woman of rank. I would consider it vulgar to offer you a definite settlement in return for your favors as I would with a dancer or an actress. Is that what you expect? You want some definite commitment from me before you will become my mistress?"

"Mistress?" she said with cold hauteur. "I have never been any man's mistress, my lord, and I never shall be. You were quite correct, Edmond. I am a woman of wealth and of rank. I do not need to sell my body either for money or for pleasure, or to satisfy some man's lust. I have been insulted enough. Kindly have your man summon me a hackney cab. I wish to return home immediately."

Lord Waite turned without a word and strode across the room to a sideboard that held several decanters and glasses on a tray. He poured himself a generous drink, but did not offer one to his companion. He stood with his back to her, drinking it. So that was it, was it? She was holding out for marriage. The impertinent baggage! She seriously thought that he would stoop so low as to marry her, the daughter of a nobody, widow of a man who for all his wealth had been nothing more than a cit. The scheming, conniving baggage. She had better start looking elsewhere.

He put down his empty glass and turned toward her. She was still standing in the same place, her chin held high, one heavy strand of hair fallen across her shoulder. God, but she was beautiful.

"I shall drive you home myself, ma'am," he said, moving to retrieve the coat that he had tossed across a chair. "Please have a seat. I shall be with you in five minutes. Would you like refreshments? Tea, perhaps?"

"No, thank you."

He bowed and left her. He returned within the five minutes, his own greatcoat already in place over his coat, her pelisse and bonnet on his arm. They exchanged not a word on the way back to Pall Mall. Only when he lifted her down to the courtyard before her own door did he finally look her in the eye and raise her hand briefly to his lips.

"My apologies, Felicity, if I have caused you distress," he said stiffly. "Good day to you."

"Good afternoon, my lord," she said.

❦ 12 ❧

Felicity had thought she was prepared for the reaction that the announcement of her betrothal to Tom would bring. But really, she discovered, she had considered only two people in depth. She had worried about Tom because the announcement would be false and he would end up looking jilted when she married someone else. And she had considered Lord Waite, though she had not been at all sure that the announcement would have the desired effect on him. In the event, she found that she was not prepared at all.

The announcement appeared in the paper the morning after her quarrel with Lord Waite. Laura was reading the *Post* at the breakfast table, as she frequently did. She was not much interested in the political pages, but she always felt it her duty to read society news and announcements so that she might keep Mama informed in her weekly letters. Her sisters' attention was caught when she sputtered over her coffee and coughed herself red in the face for a whole minute.

"Are you all right, Laura?" Lucy asked, rising to her feet and thumping her twin on the back.

For answer Laura made a few incomprehensible noises through her coughing and pointed to the middle of the page at which the paper lay open.

Lucy leaned across her, still patting her back and read.

"What?" she shrieked. She abadoned her mission of mercy and grabbed the paper with both hands. "It says here that you and Mr. Russell are betrothed, Felicity."

Felicity sat back in her chair and smiled in embarrassment. Somehow the time had not seemed right all the day before to break the news to the twins. Now it was too late to do so herself.

"Is it true?" Laura croaked.

"Yes, it is true," she said calmly. "We decided at the garden party that we would make a formal announcement."

They both gaped at her for a moment. She was never sure afterward which of them shrieked first and lunged at her. But certain it was that for several minutes' duration she was all but suffocated beneath hugging arms and eager kisses and noise.

"Felicity! I knew it! I knew it would end this way."

"But, you dark horse, you gave no sign."

"Mr. Russell! You lucky, lucky thing, Felicity, I would have made a play for him myself ages ago had he just been a little younger."

"Are you going to live at home again, Felicity? Oh, how famous."

"And how romantic. You two have always loved each other, have you not?"

"And now you have found each other again."

"Felicity, we may be bridesmaids, may we not?"

"Oh, please, Felicity."

Felicity laughed heartily. "Children, please!" she said. "I have just sat for half an hour for this coiffure. Between you, you would have it down around my shoulders again. Really, we have not thought much either about the wedding or about where we will live afterward. We are very fond of each other and wanted a closer bond, that is all." Her explanation sounded a trifle lame to her own ears, but the twins were so excited it was doubtful they heard any part of what she said.

They were finishing off their breakfast as quickly as they decently could so that they could rush to the morning room to write some letters. They came close to one of their rare quarrels over which should have the privilege of writing to Mama and Papa. Laura won on the grounds that she was their regular correspondent and it would not be fair for Lucy to write only when there was a real plum of an item to tell them. Lucy was consoled by being allowed to write to both Cedric and Adrian.

Tom himself arrived before luncheon. He was shown into the morning room, where the twins were still industriously writing and Felicity was sorting through the morning's correspondence. The twins shrieked with only marginally more decorum than they had shown in the breakfast room and hurled themselves at Tom. He smiled, with eyebrows raised, over their heads at Felicity, who gave him an exaggerated shrug in return. When the girls finally released him, he crossed to her, bent, and kissed her lightly on the lips.

"Good morning, my love," he said. "I thought you might need moral support today. It seems our announcement has caused some stir. I have been stopped in the park and at my club since I left the sanctuary of my rooms this morning. It seems to be the general opinion that I am a 'demned lucky dog,' as his grace of Newton was pleased to describe me. He even exerted himself enough to examine my worth through his quizzing glass."

Felicity laughed. "Every time Wilfred and I dined with him," she said, "he used to say he would dearly love to chase me around the dining-room table, and would catch me too if it were not for his 'demned gout.' "

The twins giggled. "What did you say?" Lucy asked.

"I used to tell him that if he did not have gout

before he caught me, he certainly would soon after," she said. "But I would always kiss him on the cheek after saying so. I always thought him a dear, though Wilfred told me that he used to be a shocking rake before the gout slowed him down."

There were, in fact, a surprising number of visitors during the afternoon, most of them well-wishers. More people than usual acknowledged the couple when they drove together in the park later. And the announcement of their engagement that very morning lent a definite air of extra festivity to the Grayson ball. Speculation had been running high ever since her return to London about which man would win the favor of the widow. She had attracted much attention, had been escorted and partnered by many men, but none had seemed to be favored more than any other. Strangely, very few people had taken much notice of the only man who was with her a great deal. It had been known early that he was a childhood friend, a neighbor of her father's, a man of no great wealth or property. He was a quiet, unassuming young man, with very pleasing manners. Most people, now that they thought of it, realized that they liked him. He was certainly not one of those many young men who would stay in a ballroom only as long as duty dictated before disappearing into the card room to suit his own pleasure. Mr. Thomas Russell, people now recalled, always stayed and always danced, usually choosing a partner after all the lovelier or more popular girls had been borne off already. Many people commended the lovely Lady Wren for being discerning enough to choose a man for the quality of his character rather than for his rank and prominence in society.

But one person was conspicuous in his absence all day. There were no white roses that morning, for the first time in several weeks. And there was no sign of Lord Waite either in Felicity's drawing room or in the park or at the Grayson ball. He did not appear on the next day either, a day that Felicity

spent at home alone most of the time. Tom had
pleaded business that would keep him occupied for
the whole day, and the twins had engagements.
They had both been invited to a picnic for young
people in the afternoon. The mother of the hostess
had undertaken to chaperone all the young ladies.
In the evening, Lady Pamela Townsend and Mr.
Booth, Lucy and Mr. Sotheby, and Laura and Viscount Varley were to make up a theater party.

Felicity did not find the day at home unwelcome.
She felt that her own affairs were getting seriously
out of hand. That impulsive idea of hers that she
and Tom should pretend an engagement had been
utter madness. She had not really dreamed that the
announcement would cause such a stir. She had felt
so dreadfully hypocritical the day before receiving
congratulations with a smile, linking arms with Tom
and smiling at him affectionately. That part at least
had been quite sincere, but she had felt so guilty
using her dearest friend in such a way.

One of the worst aspects of the whole thing was
that it was so pointless now. The events of two
afternoons before had effectively ended the budding
relationship with Lord Waite. She had wanted to
behave as a sophisticated and wordly-wise lady would
have done. She had wanted to smile mysteriously,
allow him a taste of her lips, and somehow tease her
way out of the situation. Then her engagement would
have come as a heavy blow to him and would have
forced him into action.

Instead, she had behaved like a frightened schoolgirl, panicking as soon as he treated her like the
woman she pretended to be. Truth to tell, she had
been horribly frightened. His own arousal and intent
to take her there and then had been so obvious, he
had touched her body so knowingly, so certain of
her response, that she really had lost her mind. She
had had a panicked awareness that here was a situation she could not control, and consequently had
shoved and slapped and yelled. How terribly gauche!

The strange thing was that at the time she had meant every word she had said. She had been incensed that he had forced her to *that* house and proceeded immediately to maul her as if there were no such thing as tenderness and wooing and love. The man had seemed so single-minded in his purpose. She was merely a body that he wanted to use for his own pleasure. He had no interest in knowing who she was or why she was. She had wanted more than anything to go back home and never see him again.

Now, of course, two days later, she could see the matter in a saner perspective. Lord Waite was an experienced man of the world. She knew of his reputation with women. His attractiveness, his self-assurance, left her in no doubt that he was an expert lover. If only she could have married him—too late now—she would no doubt have been superbly happy. It was just that he could not be expected to know that her own experience did not in any way match his. She really had been a frightened schoolgirl— a six-and-twenty-year-old schoolgirl, and a widow to boot.

Lord Waite could not be expected to know that her own sexual experience consisted of three aborted attempts—four, if one counted his own two afternoons before. There had been that occasion with Tom the night before her wedding, the only time she ever would have given herself freely and with love. And then there had been her wedding night and the night after. On both occasions Felicity had behaved exactly according to her mother's instructions to lie still and relaxed and to allow her husband his will. It would last but a few minutes each night, Mama had said. She had done so on both those nights, and Wilfred had kissed and fondled her until she did not know how to keep from squirming with distaste. But both times, when he had lifted her nightgown and lain atop her, something had gone wrong. Both times he had left her bed angry and breathing hard. And it had never happened again. His unfailing courtesy to her had developed into an almost paternal affection in private, a stern, possessive pride in public.

Felicity wondered if Lord Waite would appreciate the joke if he knew. He had desired a mutually pleasurable affair in which experience would match experience. Indeed, he might as well have chosen to seduce the rawest debutante. She was just as virgin as they.

However, she need not worry. His silence for two days was loud enough to tell her what she feared to know. The announcement of her engagement would merely be a seal on his decision rather than a goad to make him consider offering for her. But perversely, she wanted him more than ever. She wanted to be known as the woman who had finally tamed the womanizer.

Felicity thought the worst was over. She and Tom had faced a great deal of publicity on the day when the announcement appeared. Perhaps that Grayson ball had been a blessing in disguise. It had been a great squeeze and almost everybody of any importance had had a chance to offer their congratulations. The novelty would soon pass, the Season would come to an end, and the engagement could be quietly dissolved during the summer. By next year it would hardly be sensational news that Lady Wren had jilted Mr. Thomas Russell. The only harm done really was that the Season was now wasted. She had lost her chance to bring Lord Waite up to scratch and she was now honor-bound to stay with Tom for the remaining weeks of spring.

At least, Felicity decided as cheerfully as she could, she would have a little more time and attention to devote to her sisters. She noticed with some admiration that Lucy was making a determined effort not to mope. She had talked with far more gaiety than Laura the evening before about the picnic and this morning about the visit to the theater. Mr. Sotheby's brother, a married gentleman, had talked of getting together a party to visit Vauxhall one night to view the fireworks, and Lucy had not hesitated a moment before accepting Mr. Sotheby's invitation. Felicity was glad. She knew her sisters well enough to realize that the girl was suffering, that she was pining for the faithless earl, but she was too proud to let anyone know the fact and perhaps pity her.

Laura had been in a very thoughtful mood for the past few days. Felicity was aware that she was seriously considering the viscount's offer. She asked her about it at the breakfast table.

"I am still undecided," Laura admitted. "Sometimes when I think about it, Felicity, I think no, he would not give me the sort of life with which I would be happy. All is gaiety and frivolity with him, you see. And then I am with him and I wonder why I can have any doubt. He is so very charming and dynamic. And I see the way other girls, and even older ladies, look at him and I feel inordinately proud that it is me he is with and wishes to marry. Well, I still have four days left in which to decide, though he pressed me quite persistently for an answer last evening."

Yes, Felicity was quite glad that the worst was over for her and that her sisters were proving to be more sensible than she had expected. She was certainly not prepared for the sounds of commotion coming from the hallway as she ate a quiet luncheon with the twins, followed by the throwing back of the dining-room doors and the unheralded entry of her mother and father.

The twins shrieked.

"Mama! Papa! What a wonderful surprise!" Felicity exclaimed in delight as she rose to cross the room, arms extended.

She did not progress very far. Before she had taken more than a few steps, she was enveloped in Mrs. Maynard's arms. "Felicity, my dearest, oh, my dearest girl!" she said. "I was never more happy in

my life. Mr. Maynard will tell you that I cried and
cried for half an hour when we read dear Laura's
letter yesterday morning. You and dear Thomas.
Oh, I am the happiest mother alive."

"There was nothing for it," Mr. Maynard added,
hovering in the background, "but to turn the old
coach loose and set out with all speed to tell you in
person how happy we are."

"Laura and I were beside ourselves," Lucy shrieked.
"Only fancy, Mama, they did not say a word to us,
but let us read the announcement in the paper for
ourselves."

"We are to be bridesmaids," Laura said. "Felicity
has almost promised."

Felicity was horrified. This was how poor King
Canute must have felt when he was sitting on the
beach trying to command the tide not to come in,
and all the time the water kept creeping first over his
toes, then his heels and his ankles, and was pro-
gressing quite inevitably to his knees. How was she
to cope with this unexpected development?

Somehow her parents' outer garments had been
whisked away and they were all seated at the table,
though no one was eating.

"So we had to come ourselves, you see," Mama
was saying earnestly. "If they can become betrothed
so suddenly and without a hint of a warning, I said
to Mr. Maynard, maybe they will marry in the same
way. And they have a perfect right to do so, I said.
They are both of age. But really, Felicity, we would
hate to miss your wedding."

"Where is it to be?" Mr. Maynard asked. "All set
for a big society wedding this time, are you, love?"

"No, we—"

"Oh, do come home and be married there, Felicity," Mama pleaded. "When both you and Thomas
are from the same place, there will be so many
friends and neighbors who will wish to come and
wish you well. I want you to marry from our house,

dear, and this time I will be so completely happy knowing that it is a love match."

"I have always had the highest respect for Thomas," Mr. Maynard said. "A good, sensible young man. I am glad, love, that you have not become so high and mighty that you cannot choose a husband for his worth."

"You would not think him so proper if you had seen him the morning before yesterday," Lucy said. "He *kissed* her, Mama." She giggled.

"On the *lips*," Laura added, and snorted with mirth.

"Very right and proper, too," their mother said. "I see that London has not yet rubbed the schoolroom off you two. Papa and I are going to stay for a few days," she added, turning to Felicity. "I shall be able to help you choose your trousseau, love. You will let me help, will you not, although I know that you are far above me in your knowledge of fashion?"

"The truth is," Felicity said, trying to prevent the water from reaching King Canute's waist, "that Tom and I have not decided when the wedding is to be. We just thought that it would be comfortable to be betrothed. We may not marry for an *age*, you know."

"Nonsense," said Mama, and the tide headed for the poor king's shoulders.

Felicity left strict instructions with the butler that she was not at home that afternoon to anyone except Mr. Russell. She longed for Tom with every ounce of her being. Tom, always so calm, always so sensible, would know what to do about this horrible nightmare that was developing around her. She could safely relax and leave things with him, if he would only come. What on earth could be keeping him? She had not set eyes on him all of the day before. Strangely, it never once crossed her mind to think that perhaps he, like Lord Waite, had withdrawn from the scene, not finding matters to his liking.

He came finally in the middle of the afternoon. The butler must have warned him about the new arrivals, Felicity realized with relief as soon as he entered. He was smiling and at his ease, looking so dearly familiar and so utterly trustworthy that she could easily have collapsed into the nearest chair and let out an audible sigh of relief. She did neither.

Tom smiled at her and crossed the room to shake hands heartily with his neighbors. Mrs. Maynard caught his head between her hands and kissed him soundly on both cheeks.

"I am taking the liberty of a future mother-in-law, Thomas," she said. "I shall love you as much as I do my own boys."

"How d'ye do, brats," Tom said, tousling the hair of each twin, much to their noisy wrath, as he crossed the room to his betrothed. He did not kiss her on the lips this time. He raised her hand to his mouth instead. "Hello, Flick," he said. "I am sorry I have been gone so long, my love."

And he smiled. This time Felicity's knees did buckle under her and she sat down hastily on the love seat behind her. Tom sat next to her. Felicity's relief was not destined to be long-lived. Pleasantries were exchanged for several minutes and refreshments brought in.

"It is amazing we did not meet somewhere along the road," Tom said to Mr. Maynard. "I went home yesterday, you know, and was headed back to town early this morning."

"You were?" Felicity asked, amazed. "You did not say so, Tom. Why on earth would you go all that way for one night?"

"For the best of reasons, my love," he said, smiling at her warmly. "I wished to fetch my mother's betrothal ring. It is quite an heirloom, you know. It has passed to the brides of four generations of my family. I had to fetch it myself. I could not trust any other courier."

He withdrew a small box from a pocket and opened it. Felicity thought she would faint. All sounds and sights seemed to fade around her. There were only

Tom and this magnificent ring, a heavy gold band, set with three large rubies.

"No," she whispered, "no, you must not give it to me, Tom."

"Of course I must," he said. His voice sounded very gentle but very insistent to her ears. "You must have a ring to show that our betrothal is real, and this is the ring that my family uses. It was Mama's; now it is yours." He lifted her cold and nerveless hand and slipped the ring onto her finger.

It was ridiculous. The ring should have stuck fast on her knuckle. Or it should have been so big that it would go rattling and rolling all over the floor as soon as she pointed her fingers downward. It should never have fit as if it had been made for her.

"Mama hardly wore it because it was too large for her finger," Tom was saying, "and she would not have any part of it destroyed by having it made smaller. I am glad it fits you, Flick."

Outside noises intruded. She was vaguely aware that the enthusiastic and congratulatory voices full of love and happiness for her and Tom had been there all the time. She joined in by some effort of willpower that she did not know she possessed until the butler came to withdraw the tray, and then she slipped out, downstairs to the dining room, out through the French doors to the garden. She shivered under an overcast sky, but she was not going to risk going back inside for a shawl. She wrapped her arms around herself and became very aware of the ring pressed against her arm.

Tom found her there, perched on top of the stone wall that surrounded the rose garden, gazing at nothing in particular. "I brought you a shawl, Flick," he said. "You must be cold." He wrapped it around her shoulders and sat down beside her.

"Tom," she said, "what have I done to you? I must be the most selfish person who ever lived. I really do not like myself at all."

"No, no," he said soothingly, "don't feel like that.

It's the ring, is it? I just thought to make the be-trothal look more real, Flick. It was thoughtless of me, perhaps, was it? I really did not mean to distress you."

"Oh, Tom," she said, turning to him and hardly even realizing that she put her arms up around his neck and laid her head on his shoulder, "don't take any blame upon yourself. You are so dear and so kind. I do love you more than anyone else in the whole world."

Tom patted her reassuringly on the back. "Wear the ring," he said, "and think no more about it. The next person to wear it will probably be the wife of my heir, whoever he happens to be. Some cousin I have never seen. I shall enjoy seeing it on your hand for a while."

"Oh, Tom," she said, "what are we going to do? I had no idea we would create such a stir. How are we to get out of it?"

"If Waite reacts the way he is supposed to, there will be no problem," Tom said. "We will find some way to explain the situation. And your parents will have to admit that it is a good match, especially when they see it is what you really want. If he does not, well, we can continue as we are for a while, can't we, Flick, until the excitement dies down? Af-ter all, you do not object to my company, do you?"

"Tom!" she said, tightening her arms around his neck.

"You know," he said, "we could even get married if you'd want. It would be the easiest solution and I think we might be comfortable together, don't you?"

"Oh," she wailed, and pulled herself to her feet to stand before him. "Don't, Tom. You make me feel a perfect villain. First you are prepared to flirt with me for the sake of our friendship. Then you are willing to be betrothed to me, and now you are even pre-pared to marry me. I would never presume *that* much on our friendship, believe me. I know how much you value your bachelor privacy. I would not allow you to sacrifice so much for me. But, oh, you are so kind. Thank you for the offer. I shall always remember it." She held out both her hands for his.

He took them and smiled at her. "Well," he said, "I hope that you will get the man you want, Flick. But if you don't, my offer will still stand. Your parents have arrived at the dining-room doors. Kiss me."

She did so, still holding his hands. "I do love you, Tom," she said as her family approached across the lawn.

Mr. and Mrs. Maynard decided to stay in London for only a few days once they had been assured that there was no likelihood that their daughter and Tom would marry as precipitately and as secretly as they had become betrothed. But Mrs. Maynard did hint strongly enough that perhaps some official entertainment to honor the betrothal might be held before they returned home. A full-scale ball was out of the question. There was too little time to organize it or to send out the invitations. Besides, it was not long since the come-out ball for the twins. It was finally decided that Felicity would hold a dinner party for forty guests, followed by cards, conversation, and music in the drawing room and adjoining salons. Perhaps they would even roll up the carpet in the drawing room and dance if there appeared to be enough interest among the young people.

After dinner, while Mr. Maynard and Tom shared a bottle of port and some cigars in the dining room, the ladies worked with enthusiasm over the guest list. Some names were, of course, a must: the Townsends, Lady Pamela, Mr. Booth, Mr. Sotheby, Viscount Varley. Felicity added the names of several of Wilfred's friends, people who had entertained her much in the past and who still treated her with marked civility. With a smile, she also added the name of the Duke of Newton. She included several of Tom's acquaintances. It was amazing, in fact, how quickly the list approached forty persons.

"Are you not going to ask Lord Waite, Felicity?" Laura asked eventually, putting into words the problem that had been bothering her sister since she had begun to compile the list.

"You should," Lucy added. "He is a man of consequence and you are well-acquainted with him. In fact, I do believe he had quite a *tendre* for you earlier in the Season."

"Lord Waite," Mama said. "It sounds most impressive to have a few titles on your guest list, love. I declare I shall have the time of my life meeting all these people."

Felicity added his name and that of Lady Dorothea Page to the list with some embarrassment. The big consolation, of course, was that he would not come. She would be saved from the embarrassment of meeting him again at her own betrothal party in the company of her parents. But was it even very bad form to invite him? Would it seem to him as if she were gloating or as if she were trying to wheedle her way back into his good graces? And what if he did come? She would find the situation quite intolerable. Or would she? Would she be ready somehow to seize the second chance that this appearance would surely signify?

Thirty-two people accepted the invitation, a flatteringly large number on such short notice and at a time of year when every day presented an array of activities from which to choose. Among the last acceptances to be returned, only the day before the dinner, in fact, was that of Lord Waite. Felicity was quite stunned, as a refusal had come from Lady Page two days before, together with an explanation that she was to attend a house party in the country for a number of days. Felicity had naturally assumed that Lord Waite would be one of that party and that he was merely ignoring her card.

She was in a dither of excitement. She sought out her room immediately after opening his acceptance, about the only place where one could be fairly certain of having some privacy these days. What could his decision to attend her party mean? It could mean that he was coming to sneer, to set her down again, to prove disagreeable in some way. Or it could mean that he was curious, eager to see her again, wondering if this betrothal of hers was real and irrevocable. There was no way of knowing, of course. She would have to wait and see—more than four-and-twenty hours!

She had not set eyes on the man for a week. In some ways that was a difficult accomplishment. Normally it was almost impossible *not* to see another member of the *ton* in the course of a whole week, when everyone tended to frequent the same fashionable parks and establishments during the day and the same glittering entertainments at night. But it had happened. Of course, her own activities had been curtailed since the arrival of Mama and Papa. They were virtual strangers to the city, and she and Tom had delighted in taking them about and not necessarily to the most fashionable places. They kept country hours, and in deference to them, Felicity did not plan any evening outings. While the twins tripped off to parties and balls and the opera with a variety of willing chaperones and escorts, she was content to sit at home with her parents—and Tom, inevitably.

Felicity smiled to herself now in her room as she twisted Tom's ring around and around on her finger, a habit she had fast acquired with an article she never removed lest she lose it. Strangely, her domestic evenings and the family outings of the days were enjoyable. They were as welcome a break from the hectic round of social activities as Adrian's visit had been. Truth to tell, an unalloyed social life could be unexpectedly boring. One saw the same faces wherever one went and it was strange how eventually one ballroom began to look very much like any

other. Even the noted conversationalists could be
disappointing. At a party early in the Season she
had listened, enthralled, to the stories of danger and
adventure told by a veteran of the Peninsula campaign. She had found the accounts somewhat less
compelling a little more than a week before when
listening politely to the same stories for the third
time.

But the fact remained, she thought as she gave her
ring another twist, that she had not seen Lord Waite
for a week and that she would be seeing him in her
own home and under somewhat difficult circumstances the following evening. She had no idea if he
was still angry, or if he felt bitter or totally indifferent to her. But she did feel strongly that this occasion would give her one more chance to engage his
interest. If she allowed him to let the following evening pass without a sign, then she could be sure that
he accepted her betrothal as fact and had no wish to
change matters.

Sometimes her room was no guarantee of privacy
after all, she thought ruefully as Laura's head appeared around the door after the gentlest of taps.

"Are you busy, Felicity?" she asked. "I feared
perhaps you were not feeling well and were lying
down."

"No, no," Felicity assured her, "merely thinking
of tomorrow evening and trying to be sure in my
mind that all details have been taken care of."

"I am quite sure that Mama has not allowed you
to forget the smallest item," Laura said. "I have
been thinking of tomorrow night, too. I have promised Jonathan to give him my answer."

"Yes, it is more than a week, is it not?" Felicity
said. "And do you need my help, Laura? Are you
still finding the decision difficult?"

"A little," the girl admitted. "I have not talked to
Mama. I am afraid that she would be so impressed
that Jonathan is a viscount that she would advise me
to accept. And I do not like to dwell on the topic

with Lucy. She is dreadfully upset, you know, by the defection of Darlington. She has not said as much to me, but I know. Twins know these things, you see."

"Yes," Felicity said with a sigh, "I know, and I am merely a sister."

"I have decided to say yes," Laura said, "but I wanted to ask you, Felicity. Is it right to say yes when one is not absolutely certain sure that one will be happy forever and ever?"

"We can never be absolutely sure of the future," Felicity said. "The best we can do is use our intelligence and common sense and be as sure as we possibly can."

"But you see," the girl said, "I look at you and Mr. Russell and even I can see that you two are so perfectly right for each other. I mean, you always seem able to talk quite comfortably about any topic under the sun. And you are most awfully fond of each other. I just wish I could be that sure of Jonathan."

Felicity was shaken. "Don't compare yourself with someone else," she said. "Other people and other relationships are not always what they seem. Tom and I were childhood friends."

"Well, anyway," Laura said, "I mean to say yes and then Jonathan can talk to Papa before he leaves for home and all will be settled. Wish me happiness, Felicity?"

"Of course I do," her sister replied, rising and hugging her sister hard.

Cook had really excelled herself, Felicity reflected as the third course was borne away and the fourth carried to the table. The guests had all arrived in time, the food and wine were good, conversation was lively. The evening was going to be a success despite the presence of Lord Waite. He had been one of the last to enter the drawing room before dinner. His appearance had caused her heart to thump uncomfortably, but she had made the introductions to her parents with her cool mask firmly in place. Mama had been clearly impressed with his tall, aristocratic figure, looking particularly outstanding dressed in black with an effusion of lace at his throat and cuffs. He had been unsmiling, but his pale eyes had looked directly into Felicity's and he had raised her hand and placed it to his lips. He had been one of the few guests to make no reference to her betrothal.

But the meeting was safely over. And now he was seated halfway down the long table, conversing with the ladies on either side of him, not looking overly festive or noticeably angry or depressed. She must arrange for some private words with him before the night was out. Tom had agreed with her when she had mentioned the matter earlier in the day. He had thought it important that she talk with Lord Waite, find out for certain if there was hope or not. Tom had pointed out that they had both been angry when they last parted, and that such a parting was not satisfactory. Each of them needed to be cool and reasonable before a final decision was made about their future relationship. Tom always made sense. Felicity did not for a moment doubt that he had given good advice.

Conversation at the dinner table could not be general. The gathering was too large to make that a possibility. But occasionally one of those strange lulls in the general hum of talk made the conversation of one group audible to another for a short while. Mrs. Maynard was holding forth on her favorite topic when such a lull occurred. She was seated at the head of the table, to Felicity's left.

"And I have just thought of another reason why your wedding should be arranged for this summer," she said, patting Felicity's hand before picking up her knife again. "In the autumn we will be having a new curate. Mr. Moorehead has been granted his own living in the Midlands somewhere. Imagine, love. And him so young. But it would be so much lovelier, dear, to be married with someone we know helping to officiate. I know you met him only a few times, but he and Thomas are fast friends."

Felicity laughed and made a noncommittal reply, and the conversation a little farther down the table, involving the twins and their group of young friends, was revived when Mr. Booth introduced a new topic.

The gentlemen did not take longer than a half-hour to join the ladies after dinner. One salon was set up as a card room and quickly filled. In the main drawing room tea was served, several conversation groups flourished, and a few young ladies displayed their talents on the pianoforte. But, as Felicity had expected, the young people wished to dance, and a Mrs. Price good-naturedly agreed to play for them. The tea and the conversationalists were removed to the smaller of the two salons, the carpet was rolled up, and the pianoforte music began.

Felicity herself decided to join none of the three groups, but to wander from room to room, mingling with as many people as possible and ensuring that everyone had what he needed. She was finding it somewhat easier to mix than she had at the start of the Season. And now, as well as her customary half-smile and dreamy eyes, she had Tom's ring to hide behind, a marvelous bulwark.

Tom himself was in the drawing room, smiling cheerfully and dancing constantly. Felicity was somewhat surprised at his choice of room until she counted heads. There were two more ladies than gentlemen present, even counting Tom. Of course, he would have to stay to make sure that no girl felt herself to be a wallflower for very long, at least. It was only recently that Felicity had discovered, in a chance comment, that of all social activities, dancing was the one that Tom most disliked. Yet one would never think so to see him now. She caught his eye across the room and smiled.

"Not dancing, Lady Wren?" Lord Waite asked at

her shoulder. "The floor is rather crowded, I must admit."

"I am trying to see to the needs of all my guests, my lord," she said.

"Are you?" Somehow she found herself gazing into his eyes. "And are my needs included in that, Felicity?"

She smiled. "May I have a footman bring you a drink, my lord?"

"Witch!" he said. "Do you willfully misunderstand me? Where may we be alone?"

Felicity looked at him, her expression quite impassive. "There is the book room or the garden," she said at last. "Which would you prefer?"

"Oh, the garden, by all means," he replied. "It should be suitably deserted on a chilly night like this. Go fetch a shawl. I shall wait for you."

Tom saw them go as he gently coaxed a few stammered words from the very shy Miss Price with whom he danced. He also noticed the shawl that Waite took from Felicity's hands and placed around her shoulders. They were going into the garden. It was not all over between them, then. And Waite knew that she would not be his mistress. Was he merely going to try again, or did he have a different sort of proposal to make her? Tom felt slightly sick.

He supposed that he was the biggest fool in Christendom. He had become far more involved than he had ever intended. Led on by dreams, faint, despairing hopes, he had entered this engagement with her, and in order to make the deception more believable for her sake, he had behaved as if the whole thing were real. Touching her, using endearments when talking to her, and kissing her were self-imposed torment. His brain was constantly reminding him that all this might end at any moment and that he would then return to the country without her, alone for the rest of his life.

That business of the ring had perhaps been an act of selfishness, he had to admit to himself now. He bowed over the hand of Miss Bell and assured her that it was quite unexceptionable to waltz, even if she had not been approved by the patronesses. *He* would not tell and he was sure that the lips of the other dancers would also be sealed, especially those of Miss Price and Lucy Maynard, who had also not been approved. But look at them now! He had convinced himself that the ring would add just the touch needed to make the engagement seem quite authentic, should Lord Waite, for example, guess that it was all a ruse staged for his benefit. But he knew that the ring had been unnecessary. It had even hurt her a little to be given it. But ever since he had been nineteen, he had imagined the ring on Felicity's finger, his family's ring, his bride. No one else would ever wear it in his lifetime. He had not been able to resist the chance of seeing it on her hand for a few days, or perhaps a few weeks, of make-believe.

Tom tightened his arm at the waist of Miss Bell, bent his head closer to her, and smiled reassuringly. It was his fault that they stumbled so frequently. He must confess to her that he had never taken one lesson in the waltz. She had not, either? Well, then, for a couple of amateurs they were really not doing so badly, were they? If she could endeavor to relax and trust him, he would undertake to try not to tread on her toes for the rest of the dance. Would she? Miss Bell smiled shyly, relaxed utterly under the genuine kindliness of his smile, and discovered that waltzing was not so difficult after all.

It was so hard sometimes, Tom thought, to remember that in fact there was no betrothal. It felt so right, such a natural extension of their friendship, to be able to kiss her, call her his love, sit with her and her parents of an evening in domestic harmony. And it was very difficult to show just the right amount of affection so that no one else would suspect the truth without showing enough love to make her suspect the truth. He thought that on the whole he had done rather well. He did not believe she had detected his wild joy on seeing her again after his hurried journey home. And surely she had not detected the horrible ache in his heart that he had felt when he saw his ring on her finger and knew that it would be there for only a short time. In the garden afterward she had not known how cruelly she was twisting the knife in his breast by putting her arms around him and telling him in her dearest sisterly fashion how she loved him.

And he had been very careful earlier in the day to hide the hurt he had felt when she asked his advice about how to approach Lord Waite this evening. He had tried quite objectively to give her the advice he would have given if he really were no more than her dearest friend. The only time, in fact, that he had slipped and almost let her know the truth was that time at the Townsend garden party when he had kissed her. He had intended a mere brief touching of the lips and a close hug. He did not know what had happened. But he was very glad afterward that she had thrown herself with such abandon into convincing Waite of the passion between them. Otherwise, how could she have missed noticing that he had kissed her with all the ardor of a lover? He still did not know how he had succeeded in pulling himself free of the madness that had gripped him for a few unguarded moments.

Tom seated himself beside Lady Pamela Townsend. "Can I persuade you to dance this one with me?" he asked. "Or would you prefer that I find you a glass of cool lemonade?"

She smiled gratefully at him. "The lemonade, please, Mr. Russell. Oh, my poor feet. I thought it safe to wear new slippers tonight as there was to be no dancing."

"You know," said Tom, "I wager no one would notice if the slippers disappeared under the chair. Maybe other girls would follow your example, wishing that they had had the courage to start the trend."

"Dare I?" she asked with a laugh of genuine amusement.

"I shall go in search of that lemonade," said Tom.

How could he do this, he thought as he went in search of a footman: dance, smile, talk about nothing, look after the needs of young ladies, when his whole heart, his very soul, was out there at the meeting in the garden? What was happening? Had Waite come to his senses and was even now offering marriage to his darling? For her sake, he hoped so. He almost willed his rival to behave honorably. She so passionately wanted him and the sort of life he offered. And she deserved to be happy. He feared that her life with Wren had not brought much contentment. Yet he dreaded to see her come inside again, dreaded to see the bright look of happiness that might be on her face. He knew that he had no hope anyway, but he was desperate enough that even this interlude of make-believe was to be grasped at. Memories of these days would have to serve him for a lifetime.

Felicity and Lord Waite had been wrong in their guess that the garden would be deserted. And even Tom had not consciously noticed the absence from the drawing room of Laura and Viscount Varley. They too had retired to the garden, he confident and smiling, she with a rather set white face. Fortunately for the other pair, they chose to stroll toward the stables, at the opposite end of the grounds from the roses.

"Well, Laura," Varley began as soon as trees hid the house from their sight, "tell me what my fate is to be. I have not known a moment's rest since I spoke to you more than a week ago."

"I am sorry, Jonathan," she began.

"What?" He laughed and turned her to face him. "I am not about to be rejected, am I?"

"I am sorry," she repeated. "I thought I was going

to say yes. And I am very sensible of the great honor you have done me. But I cannot marry you, Jonathan."

"What?" he said incredulously. "Surely you joke, Laura. Why would you possibly reject me? Do you realize all that I can offer you?"

"Yes, I do," she said.

"I cannot believe this," he continued. "I was fully prepared to defy all the arguments my family would pose against the match. And *you* will not have *me!*"

"I am sorry," she said.

"May I ask why?" he asked curtly.

"I do not believe we should suit," she said. "I—I do not love you."

"Love?" he said scornfully. "What does love have to do with the matter? And is there someone else with whom you do fancy yourself in love?"

"Yes," she said almost in a whisper.

"So!" he said. "You are in love with another man, yet you have been leading me on?"

"Not quite that heartlessly, Jonathan," she said, her voice pleading. "I have tried to forget him because I thought it a less-than-advantageous match. But now the time has come to make a decision, I find that circumstances do not matter. Only the person does."

He laughed harshly. "A country farmer, I suppose."

She did not reply.

"I have been ousted by a farmer," he said, laughing again. "This is incredible. Do you realize how many young girls and their mothers have set out their lures to trap me? Do you realize how many married ladies have signaled to me their availability? And I have been refused by a little chit of a nobody in favor of a farmer with dirt on his boots and under his fingernails. Well, my love, you have something to boast of to your grandchildren—if they believe you."

"I am glad now that I did reject you," Laura said quite calmly. "I was afraid you would be upset. But I am no longer sorry. I see that only your pride is hurt. I know now that we would never have suited, my lord. There is room in your life for only one love and that love is already given. You love yourself very greatly, my lord."

Having delivered herself of this very satisfactory little speech, Laura turned and walked unhurriedly back to the house, despite the fact that the evening air had raised goose bumps along her bare arms. Varley did not immediately follow her but remained among the trees to cool his temper and recoup his pride.

～ 14 ～

"A rose garden," Lord Waite commented. "Very pleasant in the daytime, I would imagine. The scent is quite strong now."

"Yes," Felicity said, "they are just coming into bloom."

"Shall we sit on this bench?" he suggested.

They sat side by side, a little distance apart.

"Felicity," he said, "shall we have some plain speaking? We have both played games, I believe, but unfortunately I think we were not playing the same one. I thought I knew the rules and followed them. I thought that your desire to become my mistress was as strong as mine to make you so. Your early reluctance I took to be rather delightful teasing. But I had no doubt that we were aiming for the same goal. I believe I was wrong?"

"Yes, you were very wrong, my lord," she admitted.

"I have found in the past," he continued, "that young widows, when they have both beauty and wealth, relish their freedom and infinitely prefer to take lovers than to give their freedom and their money into the keeping of another husband. It is wrong, of course, to generalize, but that is what I have been guilty of doing. You seem to need the security of marriage. Am I right?"

"Yes," she said, and she was unconsciously holding her breath.

"Felicity," he said, "you know that I cannot marry you myself, do you not? Delightful as the prospect would be, I am not entirely a free man. I am not formally betrothed to Dorothea yet, but there has been an understanding between our families since her infancy. I would provoke an ugly family scandal if I were to cry off and marry another woman. What I would like you to do is to marry as well, someone with whom you can live comfortably and respectably."

"I am to marry Tom Russell," she said tonelessly.

"But that will not serve us," he said. "Russell is not a city man, Felicity. He will doubtless go home this summer and never appear again, until it is time, perhaps, to find husbands for his daughters. The marriage will never do, my dear. You and I will be forever apart if you proceed. I cannot believe that you are seriously considering it."

"We are to marry this summer," Felicity said, twisting the ring on her finger.

"And leave this life to which you belong?" he said. "And me? I cannot think you really wish to do that. Marry someone else, Felicity, someone who moves in the same circles as we do. There are any number of men who would be delighted to marry you and give you the security you need, but who would not try to put a rub in the way of our affair."

"I think you do not understand, my lord," she said. "I do not want an affair. I will be no one's mistress but my own."

He got to his feet and pushed an impatient hand through his carefully combed hair. "Come here," he said, holding out an imperious hand to her. "Let me prove to you how much you want me and need me."

"No," she said, "I will not allow you to touch me or kiss me in that way again, Edmond. I am promised to Tom. I will not make love with another man."

"Ha! Russell," he said scornfully. "He is hardly the sort of man to whom a woman would wish to be faithful. Though in the country, my dear, you may have little choice. Be warned. A thoroughly dull dog, Felicity."

She leapt to her feet, eyes blazing. "You will not say anything against Tom in my house, my lord, or anywhere else in my hearing," she said. "He is the dearest, kindest, most honorable man in the world. He has more worth in one of his little fingers than could be found in you and me put together. How dare you defile his name!"

"Well, well," Lord Waite said, a strange smile on his lips, "you will be convincing me that this is a love match, Felicity. You are quite the little actress, my dear."

"I do love Tom," she cried passionately. "I love him more than I have ever loved anyone. And I am not worthy of even a passing smile from him."

"So there!" he completed, mimicking her voice and tone. And he laughed and reached for her. "Yes, I understand you, love. You have known him all your life and have hero-worshiped him almost as long. And I daresay you are right. If I can overlook my jealousy, I believe I can admit that he is a most worthy soul. He seems surprisingly popular, at all events. But you must not mistake your feelings for love, you know. You are as different from him as day is from night. If you marry him because you are fond of him, Felicity, you will grow to hate him and he you. You belong here, where life always has new excitement and new lovers. Now, you and I will be fortunate. We may love and give each other pleasure for as long as we both wish—a lifetime, perhaps. But we will not be bound, Felicity. We will both be free to move on whenever we wish."

She had buried her head against his shoulder as soon as he had taken hold of her. He held her against him still, rocking her in silence.

"I can see that I have set up a turmoil in your mind," he said. "I shall let you think matters over for the night and see you tomorrow. Let's return to the house now. A kiss before we go?"

Felicity lifted her head from his shoulder but averted her face. "It is high time I returned to my guests," she said.

Indoors, the footmen were beginning to lay out a supper in the dining room. Felicity went first to the small salon, where she smiled at the people there talking. She tiptoed into the card room to see if supper could be conveniently served in five minutes' time. And then she went to the doorway of the drawing room to see if the dancers were ready for a rest and refreshments. Tom joined her there almost immediately as a country dance was just drawing to a close. He looked smilingly at her rather set, determinedly bright face and drew her hand through his arm.

"Refreshment time, did you say?" he asked. "Let us lead the way."

They took their plates back to the drawing room, the dining room being rather crowded with people serving themselves from the long table.

"It's no good, Flick?" Tom asked quietly as they seated themselves on a love seat.

"He still wants me as his mistress," she replied, her eyes on her plate. How had she come to take so much food, or any food at all, for that matter? She was certainly not hungry.

Tom's hand covered one of hers briefly and gave it a comforting squeeze. "I am sorry," he said. "I had hoped that things would turn out well for you. Is there no hope at all?"

"I will never be married to Lord Waite," she said. "So there is an end of the matter. Now all that remains to do is for me to set you free, Tom, with the minimum of embarrassment."

"You know you need not worry about that," he said. "I am willing to keep up the pretense for as long as you wish. And you need not fear embarrassing me. I will be quite indifferent to what people say, you know, when we go our separate ways."

She gave him a tiny smile that began to wobble at

the edges. "I have made rather a mess of my life, have I not?" she said.

"I don't see how," he reassured her. "You have had the misfortune to fall in love with the wrong man, perhaps. But you are still young, Flick, and you have this home and your fortune and your beauty. You will meet someone yet with whom you can live your life of travel and gaiety and social prominence. The world does not end with one unhappy love. It goes on. And we go on, too."

They were joined at that moment by Lucy and Lady Pamela and their escorts, and the conversation became merry before the indefatigable Mrs. Price returned to her place at the pianoforte and the dancing resumed.

Felicity was standing in the morning room, her back to the door, when Laura came in. She was reading the card that had come with the white roses, though she really did not need to do so. She turned as she heard the door open.

"Oh, Lord Waite is sending you flowers again," Laura said. "Are they a betrothal gift, or a good-bye gesture?"

Felicity laughed. "I really have no idea," she said. "You are up late this morning, Laura. I waited impatiently all through breakfast for you to appear. I half-expected last night that you would ask me to make an announcement. Did the viscount not have a chance to speak to Papa?"

Laura advanced farther into the room and sat down on a sofa. She blushed deeply. "I refused him," she said.

"You did what?" Felicity stared at her sister and plumped herself down in a chair next to the vase of roses.

"I refused him," Laura repeated, "and very glad I was afterward, too. I have always known, Felicity, that Jonathan is a little conceited, but I thought that after all he has a great deal to be conceited about.

But really! He just could not belive that I was not on the ground at his feet swooning with the honor he had done me. It was disgusting. He reminded me of all the women, married and single, who would give all their worldly goods for a chance to be in my place."

"Oh, dear," Felicity said. "No doubt he was hurt and took your rejection rather badly."

"Well, I gave him a piece of my mind, anyway," Laura said.

"But why, love?" Felicity asked. "Why did you refuse him, I mean? I thought you meant to have him."

"I did," Laura said, and sat looking at her hands for a while. "But Mama brought me to my senses."

"Mama? I thought she would have persuaded you to accept."

"Oh, she knows nothing about the offer," Laura said. "It is what I overheard her say at the dinner table."

Felicity looked puzzled.

"About Mr. Moorehead."

"The curate?" Felicity asked. "Was there something between you, Laura? I confess that when I was at home I suspected that he had a *tendre* for you. And he was certainly able to distinguish you from Lucy."

"I never did tell anyone," said Laura, "not even Lucy. I used to go to the church almost every week to arrange the flowers. I have always done it since I was fifteen. Lucy used to come too, but she did not enjoy it. Her idea of arranging flowers is to bunch their stems together and thrust them into a vase of water. She used to get impatient with me when I would spend time changing them and changing them until they looked just right. Anyway, last year when Mr. Moorehead came as curate, he used to come into the church when I was there and talk to me for a while. There was nothing clandestine about it,

Felicity. It was never for longer than five or ten minutes."

"I am sure there was not," Felicity said with a smile. She could hardly imagine the very earnest young curate she remembered behaving with less-than-perfect propriety with a young girl of his parish in his own church.

"I always looked forward to our meetings," Laura said, "and did not really give a thought to why I kept them a secret. Maybe, without realizing it, I did not want Lucy to be there too. Do you remember meeting Mr. Moorehead in the village just before we came with you? When he detained me to talk to me, he said that he wished I might be happy in London. But he said that if I came home in the summer unattached, he would speak to Papa. I was surprised. I had not really thought of him as a possible suitor, you see. And I did not know what to think."

"And Mama mentioned last night that he is going to go away at the end of the summer," Felicity added.

"Yes. And then I realized how sorry I should be never to see him again. I have enjoyed these weeks with you, Felicity, and I shall always be grateful that you brought me. I would always have wondered, you see, what this kind of life was like. But now I believe I shall return home with Mama and Papa. I can hardly wait, in fact. It seems a lifetime since I have seen him."

"Are you sure you will be able to bear the life of a country vicar's wife?" Felicity asked. "It could be very dull and monotonous, I would think. And vicars are usually not very affluent."

"Actually," Laura said apologetically, "though I mean no offense to you, Felicity, I find this life rather dull. This morning we shop. This afternoon we visit or are visited and we drive out. This evening we go to a party or a ball or a soiree or the theater or the opera. And every day the same. When does one have the chance to do anything interesting?"

"Like arranging flowers?"

"Yes." Laura giggled. "Or keeping house for one's man and making sure that it is clean and neat for him, with a hot meal on the table when he comes home from a day of visiting the sick."

Felicity impulsively jumped to her feet and hugged her sister. "Oh, and to think," she said, "that at first I thought you two were very dear but dizzy little girls! You are nothing of the sort. Both of you have a maturity and a common sense that puts me to shame. I need not wish you happy. I am sure you will be so. And Mr. Moorehead will be an admirable brother-in-law, I am sure. Go and pack your trunks, love. I shall send a maid to help you."

Yes, undoubtedly, Felicity thought an hour later as she wandered in the rose garden checking the progress of the blooms, her twin sisters put her to shame. Laura had had a chance to be a countess, to be married to a very wealthy and attractive young man. Not many eighteen-year-olds would have been able to resist the lure of such a future, especially for the alternative of being married to a young vicar who had little more than his own goodness to recommend him. Laura had the sense to realize that a busy life was not necessarily a fulfilling life. And Lucy, too, had not been dazzled by the rank of the Earl of Darlington. She had tried to consider him as a man, a person with whom she might or might not have wished to spend her life. And now she was trying, with a dignity beyond her years, to cope with the disappointment of his withdrawal. Probably no one but her two sisters suspected that she had been falling in love with the earl.

She was eight years older than the twins, yet she was only beginning to acquire their understanding of life. And it was far too late, disastrously too late. She had not even fully realized that until last night. It was quite laughable really, though she felt only like crying. She had been so convinced that she wished to marry Lord Waite, even when it had become obvious to her that he wanted her as a mistress, not as a wife. Even when he had all but forced her into that house, where his servants must have looked on her with contempt, and proceeded to treat her body with the utmost familiarity. Even last night, at first, when he had suggested taking another man's betrothed into the garden. She had had no thought at all to his character. All she had been able to see was that he was a strikingly attractive man, that he was a prominent and titled member of society, and that he could offer her a life of gay activity in London and the other capitals of Europe.

She had been totally blind, or deliberately blind, to his arrogance, to his coldness and lack of moral values. Felicity did not have a high opinion of Lady Dorothea Page. The girl seemed insufferably haughty. But, even so, Lord Waite had an understanding with her. It was understood that they would marry at some time. Yet, during the very Season when the girl made her come-out, he could be busy trying to set himself up with a new mistress. And last night he had suggested, as if the idea represented the coolest common sense, that she marry another man and become his mistress. His morality was no worse than that of a large segment of the *ton*, she knew, but did she want a man with so few scruples for a husband? If she were married to him, how would she feel when he took another woman? Would she be able to behave, as so many wives did, as if she neither knew nor cared about her husband's philanderings? Could she ever respect him if such a thing occurred?

And she had not realized until last night what a dreadful life she was trying to make for herself. How fortunate she was that he had not weakened and offered her marriage. She might now be betrothed to him, so full of the excitement of arranging a wedding that she would not have had a chance for reflection. She would have found herself in a mar-

riage far more dreadful than the one she had known
with Wilfred. At least Wilfred had treasured her and
even loved her. And there had been no question of
his moral standards.

Felicity cupped a deep-red rosebud in her hands
and bent to smell it. But she would not pluck it.
Better to let flowers grow and know their full life
span. She would not have the red bud join the white
blooms in the morning room. Oh, blind eyes! Blind.
There had suddenly been three people in the garden
last night. There had been Lord Waite. And there
had been Felicity, the angry woman who had cried
out how she loved Tom more than anyone in the
world. And there had been Felicity the listener, who
had stood back and heard the words and realized
how true they were. How could she not have realized sooner? It had been so blindingly clear to her
throughout a sleepless night. Tom was everything in
the world to her, her dearest friend, her dearest
love. How could she possibly imagine life without
him again? It would be so achingly empty, as totally
void of meaning as it had been for seven years with
Wilfred. She had thought it was excitement and social activity that was missing. But it was Tom.

Oh, how had she not realized sooner? How had
she not known as soon as she saw his dearly familiar
figure striding toward her father's home all those
weeks ago? How could she have been so blind? She
supposed that the habit of years had something to
do with it. During those first few years with Wilfred
she had thought she would go mad. She had refused to let Tom out of her mind, refused to let
a night go by without reliving in her mind that last
embrace. She had wished fiercely that he had not
stopped, that he had carried the act to completion,
so that she might have hugged to herself the knowledge that she was his, that he was the only man to
have possessed her. Instead, there had been the
dreadful emptiness, the longing, the tears. At one
time she had almost run away to him, until her

better nature had convinced her that she would be placing him in a terrible dilemma if she did so.

Finally, during a stay at their home in the north of England, while Wilfred was away for one of his rare absences from her and she had only his sister, Beatrice, for company, she had come to terms with herself. She had been married for three years. She had changed in that time, learned more about the world and the pleasures it had to offer. Tom had probably forgotten her by now, or the passion they had shared, anyway. He had probably grown in a different directon from her. She was looking to a past that no longer existed. She was behaving like a silly girl. She must forget that year of love. She must remember him, if at all, as the very dear friend he had been all her life.

Felicity sat down on the stone wall that surrounded many of her roses. She had succeeded very well. When she finally got back to Tom again, although she was free and he unmarried, she had seen him only as a friend. The arguments she had used five years before to save her sanity had convinced her so well that she had accepted them as truth. All that was missing from her life, she had taught herself, was the whirl of social activities and a dazzling, sociable husband with whom to share them.

Fool! Had she really been happy during all these weeks in London? Why had she been trying to persuade herself the whole time that if she could only secure Lord Waite as a husband, suddenly, magically, all would be well with life? Think as she might, she could remember only a few happy occasions since she had returned to London. There was that absurdly silly afternoon she had spent with Tom and Adrian, and there were the evenings spent with Tom and her parents doing nothing but talk and relax in the warmth of family love.

Would she have realized sooner if Tom had not come to London? Surely she would. Looking back now, she could realize that only his presence had kept her days bright: Tom to visit and escort her, Tom to talk to and laugh with, Tom to touch and to kiss. Oh, that kiss! Her defenses must have been very strong if she had not known the full truth there in the Townsend garden. She had known then, surely, that she had found that missing part of her life, that she was where she belonged and wanted to be for the rest of her life. Tom! Her love and her life.

And she had done terrible things to him. She had not been even a friend to him. She had used him, used the man she loved to further her own ambition, to entrap another man who really was not worth half of Tom's little finger. He had come to London to relax, to enjoy the Season for once, and she had dragged him into her affairs, forcing him to devote almost all his time to her, forcing him into a flirtation and into a false engagement. Any ordinary man would have lost patience long ago, would have turned away from their friendship. But Tom, dear man that he was, had quietly and cheerfully stood by her, aiding her to achieve what she thought would bring her happiness. And he had even offered, in his usual quiet, kindly way, to marry her if she felt she needed that support. He would do so too, she knew, although she knew equally well that Tom had settled into a happy bachelor existence and wanted nothing more than to return to it.

She did not know how to set him free without making it look as if he had been jilted. It would not matter what the *ton* thought. Tom would turn his back on London without a backward glance. But it would matter what his friends and neighbors at home thought. Many of them doubtless knew that he had been let down by her eight years before. Would they see him as a figure of ridicule or pity when he went home alone this year, without her? She felt bitterly remorseful. There was really nothing she could do to save him from whatever reactions the neighbors would show.

The only thing she could do now was quietly to

set him free and disappear from his life, so that her presence would not be a constant embarrassment to him. She would have to remain for the Season for Lucy's sake. But as soon as it was over, she would return Tom's ring, wish him well, and go home to Beatrice. Her sister-in-law was a lot older than she and lived a sedentary life in the house that now belonged to Felicity. But it would suit her. She had to agree with Laura that the Season could be very dull, quite uninteresting, in fact, if one stopped to consider the worth of it all.

Perhaps in time she would travel again, visit Cedric and Laura. It need not be a dull or a lonely future. She would be able to go anywhere in the world, in fact, except home. Except to Tom.

⋺ 15 ⋞

The day was made busy by the preparations of Felicity's parents to return home the following morning. Laura was to accompany them. She did not tell her parents the real reason, only explained to them that she had seen enough of London life to realize that it was not for her. She was homesick, she told them. Felicity knew, of course, and it seemed likely that Lucy had been told as she made no attempt to persuade her twin to stay. In fact, she too seemed ready to leave until Felicity talked with her in the afternoon.

"Is it wise, love?" she asked. "I know you are putting a brave face on it, and I do admire you tremendously for that, but really you are still pining for Darlington, are you not? If you go back home now, is it not likely that you will brood and grow even unhappier? At least here you have friends and admirers and plenty of activities to keep your mind off yourself."

Lucy sighed. "Yes, I am sure you are right," she said, "and I really do enjoy the balls and assemblies and such, Felicity. I should kick myself in the future to remember that I had cut short my one and only Season. It is just that I feel so dull inside. If I stop, I am sure I will cry my eyes out and have to go around with a blotched and puffy face for the rest of the spring. I am a silly goose, am I not?"

"No, you are not," Felicity said, smiling. "You are just a girl who has had an unhappy experience. But you have other suitors. Mr. Sotheby seems quite attached to you and he is quite an eligible prospect. Do you like him?"

"Oh, yes," Lucy said, wrinkling her nose. "He reminds me of Adrian. He is just an eager boy. I cannot see myself marrying him."

"Well," Felicity said, "maybe you should keep in mind that you are only eighteen. You will not acquire that odious title of 'spinster' for years yet. Why not just enjoy Mr. Sotheby's company even if he is just an older version of the brat? I enjoyed that weekend with Adrian enormously, you know, and not once did I think of matrimony."

Lucy laughed. "I feel better now," she said, "and I shall stay. Quite honestly, I should hate to miss Lady Jersey's ball in—what? Two, three, four days." She ticked them off on her fingers. "Everybody is to be there. Even the Prince Regent. Imagine! I have never been in the same room as him before."

Lord Waite paid his promised call during the afternoon. The drawing room was crowded. A few people who had met the Maynards in the previous days had come to pay their respects, knowing that they planned to return home the following day. Laura had written to her friend, Lady Pamela Townsend, to tell her that she was to accompany her parents, and that young lady had passed the news on to a few other people, all of whom converged on the house on Pall Mall during the regular visiting hours of the afternoon.

Felicity tried to keep her distance from Lord Waite, but inevitably he made the time to speak to her. He waited until Lord Townsend got up from her side to cross the room, and smoothly took his place before anyone else could do so.

"Well, Felicity," he said, "I did not expect quite such a circus. But no matter. Will you drive in the park with me later?"

"No," she replied. "It is my parents' last day in London. I have devoted myself to their entertainment for today."

"Ah, I see," he said. "May I speak to you privately now? There are enough people here that I do not believe your absence for a short while would be noticed."

"It would by Tom," she said. "It would be rude to him, my lord, to be seen to leave the room with another man."

"Then I must talk to you here," he said. "Have you considered what I said last night?"

"I do not need to," she replied.

"You have decided, then?"

She replaced her teacup in its saucer and looked him full in the face. "My answer is still the same," she said, "and no amount of thinking or persuasion will make it change. If ever I belong to a man, it will be as his wife, my lord. I will not be your mistress, or anyone else's."

His pale eyes looked back into hers, inscrutable in their intensity. "And you are still planning to go forward with this insane marriage to Russell?" he asked.

"I am still betrothed to him," she replied.

"There really seems no point in my prolonging this meeting then, does there?" he said, rising to his feet.

She rose too and extended a hand to him. "Goodbye, my lord," she said. "I have been honored by your visit."

He bowed elegantly and left without another word.

Lady Jersey's ball was always one of the highlights of the Season. She was perhaps not the most popular of ladies. She wielded too much power not to have offended numerous people. But an invitation to her ball was perhaps even more coveted than vouchers for Almack's. To be omitted from her guest list meant, if not social death, at least humiliation and embarrassment.

This year the famous hostess had excelled herself with the decorations. The entire ballroom was decked with pink and white flowers and green ferns, so that the overall effect was one of exquisite delicacy. Through some feat of engineering, a fountain spouted water from the center of the floor. All the French doors were thrown open. The terrace was brightly lit and decked in the same pink and white flowers. Refreshments had been set out at one end of the terrace and were being served by footmen clad in white satin knee breeches and waistcoats, white silk stockings and linen, and pink coats. Each wore a white wig in the fashion of a few decades before. Lanterns had been hung in the trees and bushes of the ornamental garden so that guests could make the most of the cool evening air by strolling along the gravel walks or sitting on the wrought-iron seats that were set at intervals along the paths.

Felicity and Lucy arrived with Tom when the wide stairway to the ballroom was already crowded with glittering, elegant figures waiting to pass the receiving line. Felicity looked proudly at her sister. Lucy looked extremely pretty, dressed in a high-waisted gown of pale blue, an even lighter-blue half-dress of delicate lace making her look small and almost fragile. Her dark curls were threaded with silver ribbons that matched her silk fan and slippers. No one looking at her slightly flushed cheeks and bright eyes would have realized that the girl was fighting heartache.

Felicity turned her attention to Tom, looking his usual quietly elegant self. She had been embarrassed, self-conscious in his presence, when she first met him after realizing the truth about her feelings for him. How was she to behave naturally, not show him by every word, look, and gesture that she loved him? But, of course, it was easy, as she might have guessed it would be if she had stopped to think.

How could one not be at ease with Tom, so relaxed and cheerful and unassuming himself? The trouble was, it was very easy to fall into the game they were playing. It seemed so natural to have him calling at all hours of the day, escorting her everywhere, using endearments and loverlike looks whenever there was an audience. It was so easy to be lulled into a sense of security, to think almost that if one held one's breath and did nothing to upset the situation, it could continue forever this way. She caught his eye now and he smiled at her with his eyes, placed her hand on his arm, and held it there, playing absently with her fingers.

"It looks like a longish wait," he said. "Will you have the first dance and the supper dance with me, Flick?"

She smiled her agreement and wondered why they kept up the charade. There was really no need of the fake engagement any longer, and they both knew it. Of course, it was sensible to wait until the Season had ended before officially breaking the betrothal, but they could already stop all the public signs of endearment. In fact, it would be wise to do so. There would be less surprise, perhaps, less scandal, when the break became official. She hoped that same thought would not strike Tom. She could not lose him yet. She needed some time to accustom herself to the idea that soon she would be alone again, not quite sure what was best to do to fill the remainder of her life. She was so selfish. Would she never learn to put Tom and his needs first?

Felicity looked in some distress past Tom, who was in teasing conversation with Lucy. She looked over her shoulder down the stairway. Lord Waite was a short distance below them, Lady Dorothea on his arm, her mother at her other side. Felicity gave him a stiff little nod, which he returned, unsmiling, and looked away, over his head, to the hall below. She had known he would be here, of course, had prepared herself to be coolly polite. She need not fear great embarrassment. He would be as anxious to avoid her during the evening as she was him.

Her eyes suddenly focused on a lone figure in the hallway, a man who had just entered the house and had not yet raised his head to view the other guests slowly ascending the staircase. It was the Earl of Darlington! She looked back quickly to Lucy, who was no longer talking to Tom. The girl had also turned to look idly down the staircase. And Felicity watched her reaction as she recognized the man in the hallway below. At first she paled, and then color suffused her cheeks. She jerked her head around to face ahead again and then proceeded visibly to bring herself under control. Within seconds they reached the top of the staircase and the receiving line. By the time they entered the ballroom, Felicity noticed with some admiration that her sister was smiling and gazing around with interested wonder at the floral decorations.

Tom was in something of a teasing mood as they stood on the sidelines waiting for the first dance to begin. Lucy had been whisked away by Lady Pamela, who had quite adopted her as a close friend since the departure of Laura.

"Well, Flick," Tom said, playing again with her fingers, which rested on his arm, "here is a whole new battlefield for you. And the Season is only half over, you know. Shall we try again to get you suitably married?"

Felicity was quite sure that her heart had slipped several inches lower, but she joined in the spirit of the game. "You really believe I should not be discouraged by one failure?" she asked lightly. "Very well, sir. My own first choice was quite disastrous. Perhaps you will have better judgment. Whom would you suggest?"

"Hmmm," Tom said. "We are still to assume that you require a title, wealth, social prominence, youth, charm, and—perferably—good looks, are we?"

Had she really been so empty-headed and conceited as to have said that? "Oh, most definitely," she said. "And omit the 'preferably.' He must be quite devastatingly handsome."

"Now, let us see," Tom said, his eye roving the room. "That cannot be too difficult. There must be twenty such in a gathering like this. How about Newton?"

She pretended to consider. "No," she said finally. "By 'youth,' I believe I had in mind someone below the age of seventy."

"Ah," he said, "why did you not say so? That eliminates a few definite possibilities. How about Creighton?"

She viewed the earl in question across the dance floor. "No," she said slowly. "By 'devastatingly handsome,' I meant someone who is so even without his corsets and his padded shoulders and calves."

"You don't say so!" he said. "And I was about to suggest the Prince Regent himself next."

"And I might have agreed," she said, "but he is married already, sir. How sad!"

"Most!" he agreed, and they collapsed into laughter that drew quite a few eyes in their direction. "Well," Tom said when they had recovered their poise, "it looks as if you are stuck with me. Let us see now. I don't have the rank, wealth, or social prominence, but I have the other qualities to excess. Would you settle for three out of six?"

"Oh, sir," she said breathlessly, batting her eyelashes at him, "may I take that as a definite offer? And did I tell you that modesty is a requirement too?"

"Then I have won for sure," Tom said, snapping his fingers above his head and drawing a few more quizzing glasses and lorgnettes his way. "Four out of seven, Flick. I defy you to do better."

They moved onto the floor to join a set that was forming. Lady Jersey, on her husband's arm, had entered the room and had given the orchestra the signal to start. There was no point in waiting for the arrival of Prinny. He invariably arrived at all functions very late and stayed but a short while.

Lucy, with pale face and set smile, was assuring the Earl of Darlington, quite truthfully, that her card was filled for the first four sets and, yes, the supper dance. But she allowed him to scribble his name next to the fifth set. She did not look at him as he did so, but smiled at Mr. Sotheby, who was waiting patiently for her to join him in the first set. The earl strolled away immediately and disappeared into the card room.

The Prince Regent arrived earlier than usual, during the fourth set. The music ceased immediately the news arrived at the top of the stairway that he and his entourage had arrived below. Lady Jersey hurried to meet him, her outrageously tall hair plumes bobbing above her dark head as she did so. The guests lined the walls of the ballroom, a buzz of excitement running around the room, especially among the younger ladies, some of whom had never seen the prince in person before.

The regent, despite an extremely portly and heavily corseted figure, still retained some of the handsomeness and all of the charm that had made him popular as a young man, until extravagance and irresponsibility and a disastrous marriage had turned public opinion against him. But all ill feeling disappeared, it seemed, when one was in the great man's presence. He walked slowly around the room, smiling and nodding regally to all the curtsying ladies and bowing gentlemen. Frequently he stopped to exchange a few words with a favored guest. Finally he danced with Lady Jersey, and those guests who still stood in some awe to watch noticed that for such a large man the prince was surprisingly light and graceful on his feet. He disappeared soon afterward, leaving behind him an air of excitement and goodwill.

"He actually smiled right at me," Lucy said to

Lady Pamela, whom she had rejoined at the end of the set.

"He actually *talked* to Mrs. Clay, who was standing right next to me," Lady Pamela said, her eyes as wide as saucers.

Lucy examined her dance booklet with satisfaction. It was completely filled. Then she remembered with a jolt that the next set belonged to Darlington. She had forgotten, in all the excitement of the prince's visit, how close it was. She glanced around nervously, to find that he was already weaving his way among the groups of chattering people, his eyes on her. Her heart turned over and she gritted her teeth.

He was not entirely at his ease when he reached her side, Lucy noticed. Good! Perhaps he would not notice her own agitation.

"This is a country dance," he said abruptly. "I shall not have a chance to talk to you. Will you sit the set out with me, Miss Maynard?"

Even as she agreed, Lucy realized that she was behaving weakly. He had really treated her quite shabbily, leaving her almost without warning at a time when he had singled her out quite markedly. And now she was meekly obeying his dictates. She should have insisted that she could not bear to miss the dance and have smiled quite unconcernedly at him every time the movements of the set separated them.

He glanced hastily around the ballroom to discover that all the seats were taken or much too public for private converse. He led her onto the terrace only to find that that too was glaringly public and crowded with dancers trying to escape the stuffiness of the ballroom, which was not helped by the scent of hundreds of flowers. He took her, unprotesting, down onto the gravel walk that wove its way with geometric precision through the ornamental lawns, flower beds, and low hedges.

"I thought you might be too angry even to acknowledge me," the earl said.

"Angry, my lord?" she asked, looking up at him with wide, innocent eyes. "Why should I be angry?"

He returned her look fleetingly. "I believe I behaved badly toward you," he said.

Lucy laughed lightly. "I really do not know what you are talking about, my lord," she said. "In what way have you behaved badly to me, pray?"

"I led you to believe, it seems," he said, "that I was about to declare myself to you."

Lucy flushed painfully. "What nonsense," she said. "Who has been putting such ridiculous ideas into your mind?"

"Your sister," he replied.

"Felicity?"

"No," he said, "your twin."

"Laura?" she asked, completely mystified. "When has Laura had a chance to say any such thing?"

"Yesterday," he replied, "when I was at your home."

"You were at my home?" she asked. She had stopped walking and was facing him, frowning. "And Laura told you that I was expecting an offer from you? How could she have done any such thing? How utterly mortifying. And, of course, the idea is utter nonsense."

"No," he said, "don't be angry with your twin. I see I have made an utter mess of beginning this conversation. Your sister was not indiscreet. She said what she did only after she knew that I do in fact intend to make you an offer. I went to ask your father's permission to pay my addresses to you, you see."

"You what?" asked Lucy, turning and beginning to walk rapidly along the path again.

"I am doing dreadfully, am I not?" he said. "Please slow down, Lucy. Can we not sit down a while?" He indicated a bench set beneath the shade of a willow tree. "I have never been in love before, you see, and I have never proposed marriage to a lady, and I really have very little idea how to go on."

Lucy sat down on the bench, but she sat stiffly with bent head and hunched shoulders, her hands tightly clasped in her lap.

"I cannot find an excuse for my abominable behavior in leaving you with so little explanation," he said. "I can only tell you the truth. I had not thought of marriage, you see, and had assumed that I need not think of it for seven or eight years yet. I was not even looking for a flirtation. And then I awoke one day to the knowledge that I was becoming markedly attached to you, that I was already dreaming of you as a wife. At the same time I considered your behavior. You are always so full of life and of laughter, so full of delight at each new experience. I did not think you shared my feelings. And I must admit, my own feelings alarmed me. They were so totally unexpected and unplanned. When my mother summoned me, as she does sometimes when she forgets that I am a grown man and entirely my own master, I decided that I would go."

"You had a perfect right to do so," Lucy assured the hands in her lap. "You are quite wrong to suppose that I was disappointed. I have had numerous escorts. I do not expect an offer from all of them. I have more sense than that, my lord."

"Lucy," he said, and one of his hands touched her clenched ones for a moment, "I was in turmoil for days. My mother wished to remind me that an understanding existed between me and the daughter of one of our neighbors. The girl is twelve years old and the understanding is entirely in the minds of my mother and hers. And I tried to persuade myself that I had exaggerated my feelings for you, that really I had just enjoyed the company of a pretty girl and that was all. I persuaded myself that you are very young and new to the *ton* and would not welcome a marriage proposal so soon. But instead of gradually forgetting you and returning to normal again, I found myself more and more obsessed with thoughts of you. I could not forget your laughter, your pretty face so full of life, your obvious enjoyment in living."

Lucy stole a look up at him, realized that he was gazing full and earnestly at her, and looked hastily down again.

"So I went to your father," he said, "and now I have come to you. I hoped to visit you this afternoon, but I had a lame horse and did not arrive home until dinnertime. I took a chance on your being here tonight. I shall not be surprised if you send me away with scorn, Lucy, but I beg you to forgive me if you can."

"There is nothing to forgive," she said, continuing the conversation with her hands. "You had not said anything to make me think that you wished to m-marry me."

"Then you will say yes now?" he asked, bending toward her and trying to look into her face.

"Yes," she said, spreading her hands and addressing her fingernails.

"Yes?" he repeated. "Do you mean it? You will have me?"

She took a deep breath, lifted her head, and turned to face him. "Yes," she said. "I love you, but I did not know it fully until you went away. I thought perhaps I was merely dazzled by your title."

"But that is not it?" he asked.

"No," she said slowly, and giggled suddenly. "But it will be awfully nice—or spiffing, as my brother Adrian would say—to be a countess."

"If you are so anxious for the title," he said gravely, "I shall have to give it to you soon. Shall I, love?"

She did not know how it had come about that she was playing with the silver buttons on his evening coat. But she paused to look up. "Yes, please," she said, and then giggled nervously as he smiled back at her for a long while.

Finally he bent his head and kissed her, an action that probably saved his button from being twisted right away from its place.

❧ 16 ❧

Felicity had been surprised and not a little disconcerted at the end of the first set, when she had been still standing on the sidelines waiting for her next partner to come and claim her, to find Lord Waite bowing formally in front of her and asking if he might reserve a dance for later in the evening. She had been too surprised even to think of refusing, but had informed him that the first free dance was the one immediately after supper.

"Please consider that my dance then, ma'am," he had said without a smile or any other expression to reveal his mood, and walked away.

Felicity turned to look at Tom. He raised his eyebrows. "Do you really want to dance with him, Flick?" he asked. "I will not have the fellow insulting you or causing you any more pain. Do you want me to deal with him?"

Felicity smiled. Did Tom realize, she wondered, that he was offering to "deal with" one of the most dangerous men in London? Lord Waite had not fought a duel in years. Anyone who was likely to have a quarrel with him backed down rather than commit certain suicide by challenging him. But it would not matter if Tom realized or not. She was quite certain that she would have only to hint to him that she felt her honor had been seriously compromised and he would immediately either challenge

Lord Waite or attempt to dole out instant punishment with his fists. "No," she said, laying her fan affectionately on his arm, "I shall dance with him. One must be civil, you know."

Later, she was reluctant to leave the supper room, where she and Tom had been greeted by a group of Wilfred's friends and had spent a very pleasant half-hour. Tom appeared to have impressed them favorably and more than one told her that she had made a good choice. One elderly lady even went as far as to assure the betrothed couple that Sir Wilfred would have thoroughly approved his successor. It was strange, Felicity thought. For those years of her marriage, she had chafed against the necessity of being almost always in the company of older people. She had longed to be with a younger set so that she might enjoy life. Yet now, with Tom beside her, she found herself enjoying the wit and kindliness of these people whom she had never really considered as her own friends.

The time inevitably came when the supper room began to empty and the orchestra in the ballroom could be heard tuning their instruments in preparation for the first dance. Tom led her back in and left her in order to search out his own partner for the quadrille. She had not long to wait. Her partner was quite close by, bowing himself away from the presence of his intended and her mother.

"Well, Felicity," he said, taking her hand in his, "as usual you eclipse every other female in the room. Did you have inside information that you were able to match Sally's color scheme so well?" His eyes traveled appreciatively over her shining satin gown of deep-rose pink.

"Merely a fortunate guess, my lord," she replied, stepping forward with him to join the dancers.

"I have reserved your time for a half-hour," he said. "I hope you are not going to force me to waste that time in dancing, Felicity?"

She eyed him warily. "It would seem the best

idea," she said. "I do not believe we have anything more to say to each other, my lord."

"Perhaps you are right," he said, "but perhaps not. Will you grant me this final half-hour? If we agree at the end of that time that there is no more to say, then I shall trouble you no more with my attentions."

It sounded fair enough. Lord Waite, for all his faults, was basically a man of honor, she believed, and a man of great pride. If she could but convince him now that there was no possibility whatsoever that she would ever become his mistress, then she would have done them both a favor. A half-hour was little enough to give in exchange for greater peace of mind.

"Very well, my lord," she said, taking his arm and allowing him to lead her through the French doors and down the terrace steps into the garden below. He turned away from the ornamental gardens, preferring to take her along the shadier path among a grove of oak and elm trees. He slowed their pace as soon as they seemed safely away from all but the sounds of music, voices, and laughter in the distance.

"Well, Felicity," he said finally, "I have to concede you the victory. You have won the game."

"Indeed?" she said, trying to keep her voice light. "I am delighted to hear it. But to what game do you refer, my lord?"

"I am going to marry you," he said abruptly.

"Indeed?" Felicity drew to a halt and withdrew her hand from his arm. Her tone was frosty.

"I cannot live without you," he said, "and the more I think of the matter, the more I realize that having you as a mistress would not satisfy me. I want you in my home, as my companion as well as my lover."

"Edmond," she protested, "I am betrothed. You are all but so. Your words are madness."

"No," he said, "I will not believe that. Nothing is written in stone. I cannot believe that your betrothal is serious. You are worth so much more than that dull fellow, Felicity, and the sort of life he can offer you. And I have not yet made a formal offer for Dorothea. I will not spend my life with that iceberg when I could be with you instead."

"I love Tom," Felicity said.

He made an impatient gesture. "Yes, I believe you do," he said, "like a sister. But as his wife, Felicity? You would be driven mad with boredom. With me you can have everything you want—jewels and fine clothes, travel, glittering company, the Season every year. And passion, love. I can promise you that. And I believe you need it. You have so much hidden fire. How could that man of yours possibly satisfy you? You would be bored, Felicity, as you were with Wren. You were, weren't you? That doddering old idiot could never have aroused your passions."

As if to prove his prowess, Lord Waite drew her close to him and kissed her, her eyes and cheeks, her throat, her mouth. Felicity stood, stunned. Yes, she had won, after all. This was what she had set herself to achieve, what she had longed and planned for. The life she had craved was within her grasp. She had only to say yes. And she felt nothing, absolutely nothing. Not revulsion—Lord Waite was a very attractive man and obviously knew what he was about. Every spot he singled out for a touch or a kiss was carefully chosen to make her feel like a woman loved and worshiped. But not delight or triumph or desire. She pushed herself away from him.

"We will be seen," she said. "There are other people in the garden."

"You are right," he said, taking her arm and strolling very slowly forward with her again. "We do not wish to start a scandal before we must. I am afraid, though, that there is bound to be some unpleasantness. I wish it might be avoided for your sake, but we will face it out. We will travel through Europe for a few months, even for a year perhaps. By the time we return, twenty other scandals will have occurred to dull the novelty of ours."

"You assume a great deal, Edmond," Felicity said.

"We must marry immediately," he said, "quietly, outside the city. I have already procured a special license. It will be better that way, one grand scandal instead of all the mess of a broken engagement for you, a family row for me, and painful announcements in the newspaper. I think we should leave tomorrow. I have property in Hampshire. We can be married there tomorrow night or the following morning."

"I believe you presume too much, my lord," Felicity said firmly, withdrawing her hand yet again and stopping to face him.

"Yes, I do," he agreed, looking into her tense face. "I am not accustomed to planning elopements. I have forgotten the most important thing, have I not? Felicity, my dear Lady Wren, will you do me the great honor of becoming my wife?"

And now that the question was out, now that he was looking at her with something like anxiety on his face, the indignant rejection that had been just waiting for an outlet refused to force its way past her lips. She stood staring into his pale eyes, searching them as if trying to see into his soul.

The only thought that would focus in her mind was that this was perhaps the answer, the way out of a situation that seemed intolerable. She would release Tom to the freedom and the quiet life he desired; she would release herself from the temptation of trying to win Tom's love; and she would behave with such scandalous want of conduct that all the blame would be upon her head and all the sympathy with Tom. And he would be able to go home contented, happy in the knowledge that he had helped his friend gain what she wanted.

As far as her own case was concerned, perhaps it would not be such a foolish move to agree to Lord Waite's offer. He was the man she had originally chosen for herself; he could offer the sort of life she had planned until love and Tom had intruded to turn all her ideas topsy-turvy. She had spent months, even years, planning for her future life, with what she had assumed at the time to be good sense. She could never have love or Tom. Once she was over the first raw pain of his loss, which must come soon anyway, perhaps she would be very sorry that she had not proceeded with her sensible plans. Life with Beatrice would become very bleak when the pain of her loss had dulled.

And Lord Waite himself was not a bad choice. He had all the attributes she had looked for in a husband, and he had just made clear his very real need for her. She did not love him. She could not feel the thrill in his arms that she always felt with Tom. But she was certainly not repulsed by him. They could be worthy companions. She could grow to enjoy, or at least to endure, his caresses. She believed in his expertise as a lover. She would be very foolish to say no.

These thoughts crowded through her mind in a flash rather than in any orderly sequence. But they were powerful enough to halt the refusal that she had been waiting to make.

"Well?" he said, a note of anxiety in his voice. "Have I rushed you too much, Felicity? Have I taken you too much by surprise?"

"Yes," she said, laughing shakily, "yes, I'm afraid you have, my lord."

"And if I give you time," he said, "will you think seriously about what I have said? Oh, I am afraid to give you time, love. I am afraid that tomorrow you will refuse to see me."

"I shall not," she said. "If you come tomorrow at eleven, I shall see you and give you my answer. And if it is yes, I shall be ready to leave the following day."

He seized her shoulders and tried to kiss her again. She turned her head aside.

"The music has stopped," she said. "Mr. Poynter will be looking for me. I am promised to him for the next waltz."

He led her back to the ballroom, where her next partner was indeed searching for her. And Tom, too, she saw, was close to the French doors, alone, looking somewhat anxious. He smiled when he saw her with Mr. Poynter and turned away to claim his own partner. Felicity was glad that there was no chance to talk to him and that her card was filled for the rest of the evening. She did not even want time to think.

The journey home was a difficult business. Lucy was strangely silent and fidgety. Felicity attempted bright chatter, but let it lapse when she realized how falsely animated she sounded. Tom looked thoughtful. For the first time, they parted that night with some constraint, with something less than the open friendship that had always existed between them.

Felicity had dismissed her maid for the night. She sat before her mirror, brushing her long hair, though the maid had already given it its customary one hundred strokes. She would have to talk to Lucy tonight. The girl was not an early riser after a particularly late night. The chances were that she would still be asleep at eleven o'clock the following morning. And she wanted all details settled in her mind by the time Lord Waite called.

Lucy would have to stay with someone else, for a few days at least, until she returned with her husband and both she and Lucy could take up residence in his town house. She supposed that as a result her sister would somehow be dragged into the limelight of the scandal, but it seemed unavoidable. At least Lucy's behavior could never be faulted. It was always exemplary.

The Townsends seemed to be the best choice. Felicity did not think they would refuse to have her sister to stay. Indeed, she thought that Lady Pamela would probably consider it a great treat. The only real problem was what to tell Lucy. For some reason, she could not face telling the truth. The girl would be so disapproving, so disillusioned with the older sister on whom she tended to look with admiration. The truth would be known within a few days, of course, but somehow it seemed easier to present her family with a fait accompli. At least then they would not be able to plead and reason with her. And she would have her husband at her side to give her moral support. No, she could not tell the truth. So, what?

An urgent message to say that Beatrice was sick and needed her? It might work, but she would hate the lies and deception that would be so obvious a few days later. She would just have to be mysterious about the whole thing and tell Lucy that she had to go away for a few days. She would tell her sister that she could not give a reason now but that all would be clear within a few days. That explanation would be a good compromise between telling the truth and lying. But she must go now to Lucy's room or the girl would be fast asleep.

Felicity put her brush back down on the dresser and crossed to the door to her room. As she pulled back the door, Lucy almost fell through it, her hand raised to knock on the door.

"Oh!" they both squealed, and then laughed.

"I was just coming to see if you were still awake," Lucy said.

"And I was about the same errand," Felicity replied. "Come on in, love, and make yourself comfortable on the bed. What is so urgent that it can't wait until morning?"

"Did you see Darlington at the ball?" Lucy asked.

"Yes," Felicity said, "and I was angry that he should appear so nonchalantly as if nothing had ever happened. Did he upset you a great deal?"

"Oh, yes, a great deal," Lucy assured her. "In fact, I think I shall never be the same again."

"Well, it is a great deal too bad," Felicity said

fiercely, plopping herself-down on the bed next to her sister. "And just when you were doing so well at adjusting to his absence."

Lucy giggled suddenly and hurled herself forward until her arms were clasped around Felicity's neck. "We are betrothed," she said. "Papa said yes and I have said yes, and it is all decided. He loves me and I love him and this is a wonderful, wonderful world. And thank you *so* much, Felicity, for giving Laura and me the chance of this Season. Oh, I am so happy."

Felicity found herself laughing and hugging her sister. "I hope you plan to let go your grip of my neck before I faint," she said. "So far, you have made no sense at all."

Lucy released her hold with a giggle and proceeded to give Felicity an account of what had happened in the garden earlier in the evening. "I would have waited until the morning to tell you," she said, "as I am sure you must be very tired. Gracious, it is almost dawn. But I had to ask you. Felicity, will you mind terribly, terribly much if I go home? I know it will seem like abandoning you, but you did originally intend to come here alone, did you not? And you do have Mr. Russell now. I must go home. I know it seems absurd when I should want to stay here for the announcement and to shop for my trousseau and what not, but I long to be at home with Mama and Laura. It will not seem real until I have seen them. Darlington thinks it is a good idea. He is going to follow me down there after a few days so that we can plan the wedding. He wants it to take place this summer."

"Oh, yes, that does sound like a good idea," Felicity said. "I can't blame you for wanting to be at home. Will you mind very much if I come with you?"

"Oh, will you, Felicity?" Lucy looked at her, eyes sparkling. "That would be marvelous. I should not feel so bad about leaving if you come too."

"Then it is settled," Felicity said briskly, getting to her feet. "We shall leave the day after tomorrow, or tomorrow, I suppose I mean. But now, bedtime."

"What did you want to talk to me about?" Lucy asked.

"Me?" said Felicity. "Oh, nothing much. I just wanted to ask you about the ball."

"Good night, then," Lucy said, giving her sister a big hug.

By a great effort of will, Felicity had slept almost from the moment Lucy had left her. And she had got through breakfast and opened her mail all with a mind held deliberately blank of everything except the matter in hand. She had decided the night before what she must do, and she dared not think until she had set the plan in motion and would not be able to withdraw easily.

It was almost a relief when the butler appeared in the morning room a full ten minutes before eleven to announce that Lord Waite had been shown into the blue salon below. She pushed the letters and cards before her on the desk into a neat pile, patted her hair to make sure that no strand had pulled free from the smooth chignon, and made her way out of the room and down the marble staircase to where a footman was waiting to open a door for her into the blue salon.

Lord Waite, standing at a window, turned at her entrance. He was wearing riding clothes and was tapping a riding crop rhythmically against his highly polished Hessian boots.

"Well?" he asked imperiously as the footman closed the door noiselessly behind her. "What have you decided, Felicity? Is it to be yes or no?"

"Yes," she said, "I have decided that I will marry you."

He flung the riding crop down onto a chair beside him and strode across the room to her. "You will not be sorry," he said. "I shall see to it that you have everything that you desire." He pulled her intimately against him and kissed her deeply.

Felicity forced herself to respond and found, with some relief, that the embrace was not an entirely unpleasant experience.

"We will leave this afternoon," he said. "We will be at my estate by nightfall. The wedding will be tomorrow morning. Can you be ready?"

"No," she said, "not so soon, Edmond. I have my sister to chaperone. Fortunately, she has chosen to travel home tomorrow. I must accompany her. I could send an abigail, but I believe it will be easier this way. If you travel a day later, I can meet you at a town or village close to home, whichever would be most convenient for you."

He hesitated. "Perhaps it would be wise for us not to be seen to leave London together," he said. "We do not want scandal to begin before it is too late for it to be of any effect. But I shall have to wait two days longer than I had hoped, Felicity, before I can make you mine. My patience is wearing very thin."

"Two more days," she said, putting her arms up around his neck, "and I shall be yours for the rest of my life, Edmond."

"Mm," he said, wrapping his arms around her and teasing her lips with feathering kisses, "I think you are a far better bargain than a certain iceberg who was destined to be my bride. And I think you will find more delight in me than in a certain dull dog you had picked for a groom. Perhaps when we are well married, my love, we can turn matchmaker and arrange a match between the two of them. Do you not think they would suit well?"

He laughed huskily before kissing her with open hunger. Almost half an hour passed before he left. They had agreed that they would not see each other again until they met in the late afternoon two days hence at an inn six miles from the Maynard home.

✨ 17 ✨

Mrs. Maynard was all aflutter. She could not remember life ever being as exciting as it had been in
the last few months. Eight years before, of course,
there had been the thoroughly unexpected honor of
having Felicity marry a rich and titled gentleman,
and in the village church too, but the glory had been
somewhat shadowed by the knowledge that she and
her husband had forced the poor girl to marry a man
who could almost have been her grandfather. And
Cedric's wedding had been a very happy occasion,
but hardly exciting. The bride had been merely a
neighbor and the marriage—a love match—had been
expected for years.

But this year! It had started with the return home
of Felicity after so long a time, and looking so beautiful and such a grand lady. And so rich and well-
set-up. And then there had been the departure of all
three of her girls for London and the Season. It gave
one such a delicious feeling of consequence to be
able to mention the fact with studied casualness
when visiting acquaintances. Mrs. Maynard had considered all these things quite sufficient contentment
to last for a while.

But now! Three girls betrothed, and one to an earl,
no less. It was almost too much joy to bear. She was
ecstatically happy for Felicity. She had lived through
many guilty and unhappy times eight years before,

knowing full well that Thomas and Felicity had had an understanding and fancied themselves very much in love. And now their story was to have a happy ending after all. She could not have been more pleased if her eldest daughter had snared a duke.

And Laura! Sly little Laura. Mrs. Maynard had been so cross when her daughter had insisted on accompanying her parents home instead of finishing the Season. After all that Papa had spent on the twins' wardrobes. She could have been knocked senseless with a feather two days later when Mr. Maynard had joined her in the sitting room, where she was placidly mending some household linen, and told her that he had just sent Mr. Moorehead into the garden to find Laura. What would he want of Laura that he could not ask of her? she had said to her husband.

"He cannot ask you to marry him, my dear," Mr. Maynard had replied. "You are married already, and I am too comfortable with you to let you go."

Droll man! But really, she had never suspected and even then would not have believed that Laura was actually expecting any such thing if the sly puss had not come in fifteen minutes later, smiling like a cat that has got into the cream, and holding hands—actually!—with the blushing curate.

Two girls safely betrothed. She had thought her cup full to running over. And then just the day after, the very next day, to be visited by the Earl of Darlington. Her heart had turned completely over in her breast. She would still swear it even though Mr. Maynard had called her a goose when she had told him. She had not been able to imagine what his business might be—had imagined all sorts of terrible catastrophes that were about to happen to them, in fact—during the half-hour in which he was closeted with her husband. And then, after he had left—a most agreeable man, not at all high in the instep—to find that he had come to offer for Lucy. Dear Lucy, her youngest girl, by twelve minutes.

And now, as if the heart were not fit to bursting anyway, to have her eldest and her youngest girls arrive quite unexpectedly, both of them looking as if they had just stepped off Bond Street. The only thing that could possibly have made her one mite the happier would have been to learn that they had driven through the village. But they had come by the other route. But no matter. That would have been too, too much this side of heaven.

The twins were as exuberant and as giggly as Felicity remembered them when she had first arrived home. After the first ecstatic welcome by Mama and the quieter, though just as affectionate one by Papa, they had seemed to feel the need for no one else's company but each other's. They huddled together in the drawing room until Mama decided that that was the best place to have tea, and after a quick cup of tea and a jam tart, they disappeared together into the garden.

But Felicity felt that she knew them better now. They might giggle and whisper together and do little to control their high spirits, but they were both sensible girls, to whom love meant more than ambition or the mere glamour of being married. Both were wildly happy, but she was convinced that each genuinely loved her chosen man.

She wished that the same could be said for her. She was in the very strange position of loving her betrothed, the man about whom her mother talked now with such enthusiasm, but of not loving the man she had chosen to marry. And two days from now she would be married again, her future irrevocably fixed, and Tom would be free to return to the quiet life that he loved. The thought was so terrifying that Felicity concentrated anew on what her mother was saying. She gave all her attention to an account of the plans that had been made for Laura's wedding in September and for her own, earlier than that if possible. Lucy's wedding, of course, could not be planned. She had made it clear to her mother that Darlington wanted a society wedding in London. But they would have the satisfaction of planning that with him when he arrived in a few days' time. It was a pity, her mother said, that Felicity herself had to rush back to London the next day and would miss the excitement of the earl's visit. But it was understandable that she would want to get back to Thomas as soon as possible.

Felicity tried to keep her mind blank through what remained of the day of their arrival. If only she could keep doing so for one more day. Once she had met Lord Waite tomorrow, there would be no going back. Then she could relax. And doubly so the following day after they were wed. She could release her thoughts then, when it would be too late for doubts or regrets. She could then think of a love that had blossomed for her twice but that was never to be.

Unfortunately for her resolve, Felicity suddenly realized during the evening that this was the last, the very last, time she would be at home. She probably would see the members of her family again, if they could bring themselves to forgive her for what she was about to do, but she could never visit this place again. And it held all her childhood memories, all the happiest moments of her life. Perhaps these thoughts would not have hit her with such force if she had found herself in the middle of someone's conversation. But Mama and Lucy were discussing weddings with some animation, and Laura was sitting a little apart with Mr. Moorehead and, understandably, they had eyes for no one but each other. Mr. Maynard sat in his worn leather chair next to the fire, smoking his pipe and looking friends with the world. But he seemed not disposed to talk. Felicity sat opposite him, also in apparent contentment. But the pain of being part of the domestic scene and knowing that she never would be again was eventually too much to bear. She got to her feet.

"I am going to walk outside," she said.

"Shall we wander to the stables?" her father asked.

Even then she could have saved herself by agreeing. "No," she said, leaning over his chair and kissing him affectionately on the forehead. "I know that when you settle like that by the fire with your pipe, you are tired and need the rest. You stay, Papa."

"Take a shawl, Felicity," her mother interrupted her conversation to say. "The evenings can be quite cool at this time of year, even if the days are warm."

She wandered around the upper lawn, admiring the rhododendrons, which were in glorious bloom, breathing deeply of their fragrance. The evening was wonderfully still and cool. She hardly needed the shawl that she held clasped across her breasts. She wandered farther from the house.

By the time she realized that she had loosened the rein on her thoughts, it was too late to stop. She was going to lose her family yet again. They were all so delighted by her betrothal to Tom. They would be disappointed to learn that she had married someone else, and without a word of warning or explanation to any of them. The elopement would hurt them, and they would be less than comfortable with Lord Waite as a member of the family. She believed he would make a tolerable husband to her if she made an effort to retain his interest and fidelity, but she could not imagine him making any great effort to ingratiate himself with her family. She did not know for certain, but she believed the man was a snob. It must have cost him dearly to decide finally to marry her when she had no noble forebears. Yes, she could certainly expect that her marriage would put a severe constraint upon her relationship with her family, just as her first marriage had. She would not even be able to attend Laura's wedding since it would take place in the village church. And it was very possible that she would not be invited to Lucy's. Even if her sister wanted her there, Darlington might feel that Lord Waite and his bride were not desirable guests for his wedding, living under a fresh scandal as they would be doing.

This was the end, then. She ran her hand along
the fence that divided the lower lawn from the
meadow. After tomorrow she would not see them
again, or not under favorable circumstances, anyway. And Tom she would never see again. Oh, no,
she must not think about him, not yet. She increased
her pace and climbed over the stile into the meadow.
Edmond. She must think of him. Handsome in an
austere sort of way. Elegant. Attractive. Impatient to
possess her. Her wedding night would be very
diffierent from the first one. Two nights hence. Exactly
two days from now she would be in his arms, probably in his bed, his wife. She increased her pace and
strode through the long grass of the meadow, hardly
feeling it scratching her legs and pulling at her skirts.

Tom. Yesterday had been terrible, the worst day
of her life. No, that was not true. Of course it was
not. But it had been a bad day. He had come early in
the afternoon to take her driving all the way to
Richmond. It was a lovely day and he had thought
to save her from having to entertain visitors all afternoon, he had said. She had gone and they had
chattered and laughed for a while until she had been
able to bear the strain no longer and had lapsed
more and more into silence. This is the last time, she
kept telling herself over and over again. And she
had desperately examined his hands with her eyes,
square, capable hands; and his hair, thick and always a little long for fashion; and his face, with
those curiously smiling eyes, and the crease between
his mouth and his cheek, slightly more accentuated
on the left side because his smile was always a little
lopsided. She had listened desperately to his voice,
low-pitched and soft, his laugh, genuine and never
harsh. And all of it she had tried to commit to
memory, knowing the task hopeless, knowing from
experience that a week from then she would be
vainly trying to recall the details and finding that
they had already blurred at the edges.

Tom had been very kind. He had asked her about

the night before. He had worried when he saw her leave the ballroom with Lord Waite and when he had realized that they were not on the terrace either. He had not known whether he should pursue them to make sure that she was not being harassed in any way. And for the first time Felicity had lied to him. She had told him that they had merely strolled in the garden, that Lord Waite had made no further reference to making her his mistress, that they had behaved as polite acquaintances. And she had lied to him about her journey into the country. She felt obliged to accompany Lucy home, she had said. She would probably stay for a few days before returning. No, she did not need Tom to escort them. He had already made a recent journey home. She certainly did not expect him to make another. She would see him when she returned.

When he had taken her home in time to change for dinner, she had turned to him and asked him to excuse her from the musical evening they had planned to attend. She had used the excuse that she needed to go to bed early so that she might be fresh for the journey the following day. In reality, she had discovered that she could prolong the pain no longer. Better to say good-bye now, suddenly, in broad daylight, with a footman holding the door of the house open.

"Thank you, Tom," she had said. "I do hope you are not disappointed. I shall see you in a few days' time, then." And then, she did not know why, especially with the footman there, woodenly staring into space, she had leaned across and kissed Tom on the cheek. The last time, the very last time she would ever touch him.

Felicity found that she was standing at the very bottom of the meadow, clinging to the fence that divided it from a grain field, staring at the corn, which was difficult to see in the late twilight. She must write to Tom in the morning before she left. It was only fair that he be the first to know so that he would have time to leave London well before she returned there as Lady Waite and before news of the hasty marriage became generally known. It would be a difficult letter to write. She put her forehead on her folded arms atop the fence for a moment.

Better still, she thought, lifting her head and straightening her shoulders, she would go back to the house and do it now. Perhaps then she would be able to get some sleep. She strode back across the meadow, the task ahead becoming more and more distasteful with every step. By the time she climbed the stile again, she was looking for excuses to delay the inevitable. She would go into the thicket, to the old oak tree. She would say her final good-bye there at their old trysting place—good-bye to home and childhood, happiness and Tom.

It was quite dark among the trees, but Felicity was not deterred. If she came here thirty years hence, she felt, her steps would take her unerringly over all the stones and gnarled tree roots that she had been so familiar with as a child. She could see the stream ahead, gleaming with the last of the twilight.

She was only a few steps from the oak tree when she became aware, with a painful jumping of the heart, that someone was leaning against it. "Who is it?" she asked sharply.

"Me, Flick," Tom said. "You would have earned Cedric's and my deepest contempt once upon a time if you had not been able to stalk us with less noise than that. You must have snapped every twig between here and the lawn."

"Tom!" she exclaimed. "What in heaven's name are you doing here, for all the world like a ghost?"

"Trying to decide if I should come up to the house or not," he said sheepishly.

"What?"

"I came all the way from London to see you and walked all this way from my own house, and then at the last minute I got cold feet. Didn't know if I would be welcome or not."

"Not welcome? By me?" she said, coming closer and peering into his face. "What do you mean, Tom?"

He smiled at her, but even in the semidarkness she could see that his eyes remained wary. "I thought you might think that I was following you around," he said, "first to London and now back here. I just couldn't get it out of my head that something was wrong and you might need me."

"I am safe, as you see," she said softly.

"It was yesterday and the day before," he said. "I cannot quite put a finger on it. It was as if there were a brick wall behind your eyes. It's none of my business, of course. You need not confide in me. But you always have, Flick. We have always shared our thoughts, haven't we? Is there something bothering you that I can help with?"

"No, Tom, of course not," she said, laying a hand lightly on his chest and removing it quickly again. "Oh, yes, I must tell you. I should have told you yesterday. I was going to write to you tonight, but now I must tell you. Tom, I can't believe you are really here. This is like a dream." She had begun to pace the banks of the stream in agitation.

"What is it, Flick?" he asked quietly, not moving from his position against the tree. "What is making you unhappy?"

"I have to go away," she said, "tomorrow. I can't stand it any longer, Tom, this uncertain existence, this living of a lie. I cannot wait until the end of the Season to let everyone know that our betrothal is not real. It is not fair to you. So I am going. You can be free to do what you wish, Tom. I know you do not enjoy London. Here. I will give you your ring now and then I will not have to entrust it to a messenger."

"Leave it on your finger, Flick," he said. "I would not want it lost in the darkness. Where are you going?"

"I am going back home," she said. "Beatrice is sick. Oh, no, that is not true. I am going there to live until I have decided what I want to do. No." She stopped in front of him and gazed despairingly at him. "No, I cannot lie to you, Tom. You would know, anyway. I cannot tell you where I am going. That is all. You will know soon enough."

"It is Waite, isn't it?" he said tonelessly. "He has persuaded you after all. You are going to become his mistress."

"No," she said.

"Oh, Flick," he said, grabbing her arms and holding on to them so that she winced, "please don't do that. You are so lovely and have so much more than mere physical beauty. You have so much to offer. You do not need to be any man's mistress. Least of all his. He is a man who has thought of nothing but the gratification of his desires all his adult years. He will discard you in a moment once he has become tired of your devotion."

"It is not what you think," she said, spreading her hands on his chest and looking earnestly into his darkened face. "But I have to go, Tom. It is time. Don't try to hold me back. I am very vulnerable at the moment."

"Do you love him so much," he said, laying the backs of his fingers against her cheek, "that you will give up all your dreams, Flick? Better to marry me. At least you would be assured of being treated with the proper respect."

"Tom," she whispered, "don't. Please don't."

"Oh, God!" he said violently, and pulled her against him so that her face was lost against the folds of his neckcloth. "Don't do it. Marry me. Would it be so terrible? You like me, Flick. You could be comfortable with me. I could take you to London sometimes. We could travel if you wished. Just don't do what you plan to do. God, I can't stand the thought of that man's hands on you."

"Tom," she said, pulling her head away from his shirtfront and looking into his face. His name came out on a sob.

His mouth came down on hers, open, demanding.

His tongue pushed past the barrier of her teeth and plundered the warm inner recess of her mouth. She was crushed to him, her breasts flattened against his waistcoat by hands that splayed across her back and held her fiercely. But he did not need to do so. Felicity responded with a wild passion of her own. He was no longer Tom, her friend. He was not even Tom, the man she loved above all others. He was Tom, the lover of eight years ago, the lover of her life, the other half of herself. And as her hands moved to his shoulders and his neck and his hair, she did not care that tomorrow she must leave him, that the day after that she would be another man's wife. She did not care that she had the rest of a leftover life ahead in which to relive this moment and mourn for her lost love. She cared only that Tom's arms were around her, his body pressed to hers, his mouth on hers. Tonight, this moment, was life, all of life, and she would live it.

She sobbed when his mouth moved away from hers to travel along her throat to the pulse there.

His hands moved around to cup her breasts, to push impatiently at her shawl, and to lower the shoulders of her low-cut gown until the sleeves slipped down her arms and he was able to hold her breasts in his hands, caressing them and kissing them.

"Don't cry," he was saying, "don't cry, my love. It will be all right. I shall make it all right for you. Don't cry." And he was holding her head, gently kissing away the tears, murmuring endearments.

"Tom," she whispered against his mouth, "make love to me."

He put his arms around her and held her, her naked breasts crushed against his coat. She waited for his rejection, waited for his return to self-control. She was back to eight years before, except that this time she knew the outcome. She closed her eyes and waited for the end.

He loosened his hold, felt for the ribbon that held

her dress firm beneath her breasts, and tugged it loose. The light silk fabric fell away to the ground, leaving her clothed only in the lower half of her chemise. Tom kissed her softly on the mouth as he shrugged out of his evening coat. Then he stooped and spread it on the ground, took Felicity and laid her down on top of it. She lay still as he unclothed first her and then himself. Then she reached for him.

Tomorrow was gone, as unimportant an element of time as the past. Only tonight, now, mattered, this moment of love with Tom. There was not a second of doubt or of fear or even of unhappiness in her as his hands and his lips and his tongue knew her in the darkness. She was to have one of the great wishes of her life fulfilled, and she was content. Tom was to be the first man to possess her. When their mounting passion set them to reaching for each other, she held his weight on top of her and took a long gasp of air, waiting for the moment that had been denied her for eight years.

Tom's need for her was great. He did not enter her with caution. He did not know there was need. He pushed inward urgently, knowing the truth only when it was too late to save her from the gasp of pain and involuntary cry.

"Oh, my God," he said. "Oh, my God, Flick."

"No, don't stop," she cried, "don't stop, Tom." And she dug her fingernails into his back in her urgency.

The only time, the last time, she thought with mounting triumph as Tom thrust again and again into her, until she could think no longer, but could only cling and arch upward against him until everything burst around her and she was no longer one-half of her being and he the other, but they were finally one whole.

She was lying on the ground, still on his coat, cradled against his warm, damp body, her dress and her shawl half-pulled around her for warmth when

she came to her senses. She did not know how
much time had passed or where she had been during that time. The moon had risen. She could see
Tom beside her, his eyes open and looking into
hers.

"Thank you," she whispered.

"Thank you?"

"You knew that I needed you then, did you not?"
she said. "And I always wanted you to be the first,
Tom. Now I will always have this to remember."

"I still don't know how I come to be the first,"
Tom said, "but that is not as important as that I be
the last. We will be married here before we go back
to London, if you want to go back, that is."

"Tom," she said with a smile that was still soft
and sleepy, "I did not ask you to do that so that I
might trap you into marriage. I needed it so that I
could set you free."

He raised himself on one elbow and frowned down
at her. "What are you talking about, Flick?" he asked.
"You just gave me your answer. You are my wife
now, even if the ceremony is to come after the wedding night."

"No, it is all right," she said. "You need not feel
honor-bound to marry me, Tom. You did not seduce
me. I seduced you." She lifted one arm and laid her
palm against his cheek. "I know that you like your
quiet bachelor existence here. You have assured me
several times that you are not on the lookout for a
wife. I will not be a burden to you, Tom. I love you
too much for that. And you need not worry. I am
not going to be Lord Waite's mistress. I am going to
be his wife."

She drew her hand away quickly when she saw
the look on Tom's face. For the first time in her life
she suddenly felt a blind terror of him. For one
moment she thought he was going to strike her.

"You can forget that notion," he said in a voice so
quiet with menace that she barely recognized it as
Tom's. "Do you think I would take my pleasure of

you, Flick, and return to my bachelor life all the
more cheerful because I had someone to whom to
turn over my leavings? I just took possession of you,
my girl; I just made you my wife. And another man
lays hands on my wife over my dead body. You may
not love me as I love you, Flick, but I am not persuaded you love Waite either. You could not have
given yourself to me if you did. I am sorry if you are
disappointed, if you really don't want to live with
me for the rest of your life. But it's too late now. You
have my betrothal ring on your finger and you have
just consummated a marriage with me of your own
free will. You won't get away from me now. And if
Waite wants to argue the point, he can name his
weapons and meet me at any time."

"Tom," she said. She was lying very still. "Do you
love me?"

"Of course I love you," he said angrily.

"No," she said, "I mean, do you *love* me? Do you
feel that you are not quite living when you are without me, as if you are only half a person and as if
only I can make it all complete? Do you, Tom?"

She watched the smile spread slowly on his face.
She knew his eyes were smiling, though they were
shadowed by the darkness. She could see the creases
beside his mouth, the one on the left deeper than
the other. His teeth looked very white in the darkness.

"How can you describe it so well?" he asked.

"Because I am the other half, idiot boy!" she cried
happily.

"I had forgotten that nickname," he said in surprise. "That's what you called me just before I pushed
you into the stream."

"And all these years I have been inclined to think
it was poor Cedric," she said.

"Flick," he said, his face suddenly sober again.
"Oh, my love, is it true?"

"Would I have let you do this," she said, spreading her arms on the ground, "if it were not?"

And suddenly they were both sitting up, hugging,
kissing, laughing at nothing at all.

"Oh, my goodness," Felicity cried suddenly. "Heavens! Mama and Papa will have a search party out for me. Tom, someone could be here any moment. Where are my clothes? What will they think, Tom? My hair is all about my shoulders. I will never find all the pins in the darkness. Oh, help me."

"Take it easy," he said, a laugh in his voice. "We will not look that bad, but bad enough that they will perfectly understand when we tell them that we wish to be married next week."

"Next week? Do we, Tom? But I can't. I am marrying Lord Waite the day after tomorrow. I mean. . . . Oh, dear."

"There is your other shoe," Tom said. "Do you have everything else? All right, love. A nice sedate walk back to the house, please, and tell me all these ridiculous plans you have made. I'll see to everything. But just *tell* me. Don't panic all over me."

"Oh, Tom," she said, grasping his arm and relaxing against it, "if you just knew how I have longed to lean on you entirely. I am not at all the strong, independent widow that many people take me for. Can I really leave everything to you? I don't have to worry any longer?"

"All you have to worry about is whether we can have those six children before you are thirty. There *are* twins in your family, after all."

"Oh, Tom," she said, laying her cheek down on his shoulder, "I do love you so."

He shook off her arm and put his own around her waist, drawing her close as they walked on. "At the risk of being very repetitious," he said, "that goes for me too, my love."

The sensuous adventure that began with

SKYE O'MALLEY

continues in . . .

He is Skye O'Malley's younger brother, the handsomest rogue in Queen Elizabeth's court . . . She is a beautiful stranger . . . When Conn O'Malley's roving eye beholds Aidan St. Michael, they plunge into an erotic adventure of unquenchable desire and exquisite passion that binds them body and soul in a true union of the heart. But when a cruel betrayal makes Conn a prisoner in the Tower, and his cherished Aidan a harem slave to a rapacious sultan, Aidan must use all her skill in ecstasy's dark arts to free herself—and to be reunited forever with the only man she can ever love. . . .

**A breathtaking, hot-blooded saga
of tantalizing passion and ravishing desire**

Coming in July from Signet!